The Marshmallow Show is Cancelled

DEBBY REGAN

Copyright © 2023 Debby Regan

Cover art by Cody Sexton of Anxiety Press
Editing by author Remo McCartney
Additional formatting design by editor Paige Johnson

www.Outcast-Press.com

(e-book): ASIN: B0CN7HDSZ9
(print): ISBN: 978-1-960882-07-3

F♥NLEY

Marshmallow: I have to hide these marshmallows from Sugar Sam! He's crazy for them!

Sugar Sam: Hi...bunny! Do you have a marshmallow today? I could really use a marshmallow. I'm craving them!

Marshmallow: Oh, hi! I'm sorry, Sam, but I'm all out.

Sugar Sam: Oh, gee whiz. Oh my, that won't do, nope. I need sugar, do you have anything? I'd even eat black licorice. I'll do something nice for you. I'll trade carrots, I'd do that. I'd do anything you want, please help me, gotta have it. I need it.

Marshmallow: Sugar Sam, if you eat too many sugar sweets, you'll get sugar sick! I'll give you just one marshmallow. Just one.

Sugar Sam: I can't eat just one marshmallow! Oh, no! I can't do anything like that. You can't stop at just one marshmallow! Oh, dear! Oh my!

The first time Finley performed the Marshmallow voice, he played to the world's toughest audience: his father. He looked in the mirror like Marshmallow's opening bit on the show. She always held a lipstick tube midair, as if she were applying it. She would stop and say, "No bunny is prettier!"

He'd taken his mother's lipstick to do the bit perfectly. His voice sounded similar to Marshmallow but a bit more neurotic, more insecure. Less confident, more obnoxious. Finley felt very pleased with his 12-year-old self until he realized Father was in the doorway.

"You're not really interested in wearing lipstick, are you?"

Finley wanted to say no. But so what if he were? The man who had spent decades as a female bunny on television was now questioning *his* masculinity? Why couldn't Father just see that Finley was talented in his own right and be supportive?

But, somehow, he already knew his father was deeply insecure. Kevin Luker held that audience as Marshmallow, and he *needed* that audience.

Finley thought about telling Father all that but only ended up saying, "No way. It was just for the bit. You can give this back to mom." His father grabbed the lipstick, and Finley could see a smirk forming at the edges of his father's lips.

As his father's footsteps disappeared down the hall, Finley washed his hands to calm himself down. He could hear his parents in the shag-carpeted living room, his father concerned about the lipstick. Something in Finley screamed that he couldn't let his father win this time.

He rushed out to confront Kevin but paused when he saw his mother clinging to his father like a child with a rag doll.

His mother turned towards Finley with an anxious face. "Don't cause trouble, Finley. Your father doesn't get many weekends off." She patted Kevin's arm, and Finley felt disgust.

Finley couldn't remember every detail, but he'd seen his mom's slipper on the floor. He must have picked it up and thrown it at his father's face.

Kevin pretended nothing had happened and turned back towards the rerun of *MacGyver*.

Finley's mother said something, but Finley didn't respond. Finley ran into his room and cried.

He must have needed water later; he put on sunglasses to disguise his red eyes. When he stepped into the hallway, his father approached him.

Finley stopped, but he couldn't think of anything to say.

Kevin stood for a deafening moment of silence, then put a finger close to Finley's face. "You will *never* throw a shoe at me again. Our camping trip just got cancelled." His father walked away.

Finley reflected that his father had plenty of time to calm down, and the response had been cold and deliberate. Inhuman.

Nothing else.

Something seems off today on set, but Finley can't figure out what. The props look the same, the Marshmallow puppet and the Sugar Sam puppet lie in a heap on a coffee table in the green room as usual, but the director and the puppeteer haven't shown up.

Dave, the camera guy, sits in a folding chair, eating a bear claw. "I'm sorry, man," Dave says as soon as Finley walks up.

"What's going on today?" Finley sits on an ancient green couch.

"You didn't hear it from me, but I think your stepmother sold the rights to *The Marshmallow Show*. The show's cancelled. Someone in Vegas bought it. They probably want you to go out there. You might want to start auditioning. Get some things lined up." Dave loves to talk and never minces words, so Finley has no trouble believing him.

"Jennifer got the house; she got the show after Dad died. What do I get?" Finley asks, but he doesn't expect an answer.

"I've heard the original puppet is yours," Dave says in a factual tone.

Finley waits for the therapist to call his name. Surrounded by concerned parents with adolescents who desperately wish they were somewhere else, he turns to the decade-old *Newsweek* on the coffee table. Of course, there's a review of *The Marshmallow Show* buried in the back pages. "Manic" and "Unpalatable to anyone over the age of 12," sneers the reviewer. His father usually pasted unflattering reviews in what could only be described as a nightmare board. Visceral memories flood Finley. At least he has a starting point to talk with Melissa today.

He usually prefers female therapists. He can only focus if the therapist is attractive. Sort of like a trick he would pull in college. He imagined having crushes on remotely attractive female professors to help him pay attention to what they were saying. When faced with male professors, he invented convoluted backstories involving family crimes.

He puts on a sad face to elicit sympathy from Melissa. He's been doing it so long, it has become automatic.

"My whole life, it's been this and that. I may have been the first born, but my father already had a favorite child: Marshmallow. And it's like she had all the marshmallows, and I didn't have any. She was the star of the show, and I was just an extra with a few lines. Dad didn't notice me because he was either with Marshmallow or his mistress."

Finley pauses and tries to remember his childhood. He turns to look at the painting above Melissa's desk, as he often does. The unknown artist meant to create a soothing, generic meadow scene, but Finley could swear he sees a rabbit in the shadowy corner. He takes a moment. The sounds of a silver wall clock ticking and the whooshing of Melissa's desktop zen fountain grows louder.

Melissa clears her throat a bit and folds her manicured hands in her lap. She smiles and waits for Finley to continue.

Finley resumes, "Then he left to be with his new wife. Mom didn't notice me. She was busy watching reruns of *The Marshmallow Show* because she missed Dad. Well, *The Marshmallow Show* is cancelled, and I need to move on with life. Only Dad isn't here anymore to see it. I'm not only cancelled, I'm ineligible for syndication. I'm the bunny with the smallest pile of marshmallows in the room." He concludes what could pass as a comedy monologue, if it had been performed in a club instead of a therapist's office, but he gets no applause.

"How are you feeling today, Finley?" Melissa leans forward, steepling her fingers.

"I just told you." Didn't she hear anything he'd said?

"No, I think that was a comedic monologue. How are you feeling? This is not an episode of *The Marshmallow Show*, and I'm not the audience."

"I'm feeling sad and discouraged. I'm an out-of-work entertainer, aren't I?"

"But you're going to Vegas to work on that?"

"It's not a sure thing. Not a done deal. That's what's driving me crazy." Finley leans back and exhales.

"Sometimes, we have to step out in faith, if you will, and I believe you're ready to do just that. I'm graduating you from therapy. Next week will be our last session. I'm very proud of your progress, Finley!" She recrosses her legs and gathers papers into his file. She often wears business separates with a creative flair. Today, its navy polka dots and sensible suede boots.

Briefly distracted by her collar bone and casually unbuttoned blouse, he registers that unfamiliar phrase: graduated from therapy.

Is Melissa abandoning him? What should he do now? Move to Vegas and beg Sparkle, Inc. for a job?

He barely focuses on scheduling his last appointment after two years of therapy. He won't miss the sight of that snobbish male receptionist in a bowtie.

The receptionist half-smiles at him once again. "We'll file your paperwork and send you the bill shortly. Have a wonderful day, Mr. Lucker." He looks down at the papers and scribbles something on one.

Finley refuses to respond to the man's continued mispronunciation of his last name and walks out the office door for the last time.

The world has flipped on its axis again, and he's hopping with his cottontail too close to a cliff.

The Mustang sputters in the desert. Has Finley really missed seeing the bright orange gas light? Would it matter to anyone if he dies out here? The cacti refuse to answer him.

That damn bunny in the passenger seat seems to smirk. "I wouldn't have run out of gas because Father loved ME!"

He must be losing his mind, writing lines for a cancelled show. At least Sparkle, Inc. couldn't repossess the original puppet, even if they now owned the rights to *The Marshmallow Show*. Waves of shame wash over him, tangible vestiges of publicly losing his temper. His throat still hurts from screaming at the director. And, oh yeah, he'd thrown that bunny off stage by her ears for emphasis, something he'd yearned to do his entire childhood.

Well, he'd already been punished for the outburst. Why should he feel guilty at this point?

The pink-and-white nightmare of THAT BUNNY haunted his childhood nursery like a parasitic twin. He could see the tableau in his mind's eye: his mother rocking back and forth, eyes as glassy as the puppet's, pupils fixated on the show perpetually onscreen—a reminder of his father's presence. His father "rewarded" that devotion with adultery and divorce. Family life became wrapped in the tissue paper of a pretend normalcy, an unwanted gift shoved into his hands like a silver spoon.

It didn't matter that his father was a man who spent his professional life in falsetto tones. The snowy white and feminine Marshmallow was the actual breadwinner in the family. The irony being that, behind the voice, his father reveled in every toxic, masculine behavior. It's possible he created the character to vent his passive aggression to the world behind a cute, bunny-shaped bullhorn.

One cannot hate an idea, or a lifeless thing filled with sawdust. But Marshmallow was a looming personification of Finley's father, complete with her own merchandise. For years, rows of Marshmallow plush bunnies flanked The Cabbage Patch Kids at every local Kmart.

It was as if Father had commoditized his very soul and made it second-rate. Meanwhile, Finley's own Marshmallow plush grew mangy as he mercilessly chewed the bunny ears to self-soothe. He hid the fact that he slept with stuffed animals from his peers in elementary school. He knew they would mercilessly torment him. Like the fictional boy's velveteen Rabbit, Marshmallow had "become real" in a way, but Marshmallow didn't have the good manners to hop away forever into the forest.

Finley should be searching for a gas station, but he can't bring himself to do it. Grabbing the tequila, he takes swig after swig then sets up camp on the side of the road. He'll use that damn bunny as a pillow.

Ruminating at Spago over the best $100 cheeseburger of his life, Finley Luker suffers equally from jet lag and angst. But viva Las Vegas (and happy hour pricing)! He's also impressed by the friendly but nonintrusive manner of the bowtied, bespectacled waiter who brings him an old fashioned. How many hours had he entertained himself in Sin City over Chinese noodles, waiting for his father to finish a show?

And his father, long dead, still shadows Finley's career and identity. The Art Deco comfort of his black velvet seat does not console him or erase his bad memories, but his back feels better.

It's not that his father missed his birthday parties. It's not that every Saturday was another recorded episode of *The Marshmallow Show*, or that Marshmallow herself loomed over the household like a favored sibling. It was all those facts that added up to the lunacy.

It's getting better, isn't it? Even classic movies die away into distant memory. But the silver lining is that are fewer terrible Bogie impressions by terrible comedians. Fewer people scrunching their foreheads before mouths emit Cagney's "You dirty rat!"

The Marshmallow Show is fading into nostalgia, only an echo of the 1990s. A vision of the TV chimpanzee, Lancelot Link, pops into his head and he can still hear the bad voice-over. He shudders. His father's show, thank God, never sunk to those depths.

She had never been real, he marveled. A puppet of felt and sequins had wreaked havoc on his psyche. He knew what she would say, "What about ME?! Well, you'll never be fabulous. I sparkle, and the audience sparkles back at me. If you SHINE, the world shines with you. Don't be silly, darling!"

The voice he imagined was not a puppet's voice. It was his father's falsetto. As he'd heard for decades. As he heard coming from his own throat since that damn reboot.

He is Marshmallow, the only Marshmallow bunny left in the world.

Unless Sparkle, Inc. replaces him, that is.

Sparkle, Inc.

Sparkle, Inc. would never be Disney, but that wouldn't stop them from trying. The whole company's history reads like a list of near successes. The founder worked with Hanna on a comic, but Barbera took his place. Mr. Sparkle almost thought of limited animation before that terrible Dr. Seuss film "introduced" it in the '50s. Mr. Sparkle almost came out of the closet first, but Rock Hudson beat him to it. As it is, a fossilized Mr. Sparkle, complete with his signature powder-blue ascot, could sometimes be seen venturing out into the Vegas sun.

The fate of the business now resides in his daughter Andrea's hands...

Andrea walks quickly in heels to meet Finley Luker, voice of Marshmallow the Bunny. Purchasing *The Marshmallow Show* had almost been an afterthought. Sure, it had played well in the '90s and nostalgia creates consumers. Having the rights to enduring characters is a steal, and Mr. Sparkle always loved that goddamn bunny. On many Halloweens, Andrea had seen her father dressed up in the Marshmallow hot-pink mermaid dress from the first season.

Now, Andrea envisions a new dawn for *The Marshmallow Show*. They would have to discard the old humor. Nobody would get jokes about goddamn showtunes. Whimsy is as dead as her sex life. Whimsy is outdated. That bunny is hers to silence and sell as she sees fit, but she'll have to deal with Finley Luker first.

"Mr. Luker?"

The stunning brunette in the navy pencil skirt speaks to him as he's mid-bite.

He finishes his bite. "Ms. Rizzo." He stands as she takes a heavily cushioned seat.

The waiter takes her drink order: Johnny Walker Blue on the rocks. "We're sorry to inform you that *The Marshmallow Show* is cancelled. We'd like you to stay and finish your voiceover work here in Las Vegas, and of course, we have a complimentary ticket to *An Evening with Mr. Sparkle* on Saturday." Andrea takes a deep breath after breaking the news.

His cheeseburger lands in his gut like a smoked cheddar rock, a particular tragedy since cheeseburgers are a rarity in his runner's health regimen. "Why the cancellation?"

"It's not the rumors that you're difficult. I just want that goddamn bunny to shut her mouth. Beyond that, I hope you'll collaborate on The Marshmallow Bunny Official Website." Her words, meant to carry considerable sting, please him, and he can't help but smile at her heavy Long Island accent and serious manner. Her hands seem to fly when she speaks.

After all, he wants that bunny to shut her mouth more than Andrea could ever imagine.

"May I buy you another drink?" Finley begins with an old line. He gives up on salvaging his professional life for the day, but he decides to take a shot with the bright-eyed woman in front of him.

"What's your angle? It's not going to save Marshmallow."

"Do I need an angle to buy a beautiful woman a drink?"

She glances over her lashes, considering. He's blue-eyed and skinny, after all. "I'd like that. Very much."

"A little lower. It brings out my eyes."

Scott struggles a bit while styling the toupee this morning. Glancing at Chas's reflection, the white vanity lights reveal Mr. Sparkle at his most vulnerable time of the day. A star never leaves the house looking anything less than a star. Joan Crawford may have been wrong about morals, but she got that part right. She also had the eyebrows of the century, and Scott keeps that in mind with a black-and-white photograph taped to one of three gilded mirrors. He taps excess powder out of the brush, onto the compact, and fills in a little on Chas's left arch for drama.

"Am I losing weight?"

"A little," Scott says, but he can't really tell.

"It's the fish oil I've been taking. Works wonders! The doctor at that Lake Tahoe party said so. The one Ed Begley Jr. introduced me to."

"Your pores are very small this morning."

"It's Joan's ice cube trick." Chas winks because that isn't true. "That's why she got the Oscar."

Scott almost forgets to glance at the other photo on the vanity. A picture of the man who broke Chas's heart but also gave him the mustard seed that grew to become Mr. Sparkle. The man known by that gossamer moniker: Liberace. "Tell me the story, again," Scott asks as he sprays a section of the toupee with Aqua Net. The story is a mantra. Positivity is all the rage.

Chas stares in the mirror for a moment then begins, "We saw *The Jungle Book* in his home theater, and I couldn't stop looking at that orangutan or Liberace. And the orangutan starts singing about wanting to be like 'you.' Why wouldn't an orangutan want to be like Liberace? It could play the piano, swing music, get it? And I put the orangutan in a black rhinestone suit with the cravat Lee wore. I started drawing the Mr. Glitz comic from that day forward. Lee never took me out again, but I'll never forget him. Ever."

Scott turns away; he doesn't know why the story makes him tear up. If only he'd been old enough to hear Liberace in concert!

Waking up under leopard-prints, shirtless Finley blinks at the sunlight filtering through a set of velvet curtains. Andrea has gone into work; the note written on Sparkle, Inc. stationary confirms this. **"Enjoy breakfast! You could eat."** He should get back to running in the mornings and drinking a protein shake afterwards, but the note and the aroma of cheese Danishes convince him otherwise.

He showers in an incongruous ivory and gold bathroom, nervous about meeting Andrea's father, Mr. Sparkle himself, over breakfast. However, he sees only Scott seated in the dining room, a marvel of 1970s glamour and French style. The mirrored walls and chandeliers seem to make even the gold flatware sparkle.

A beagle wags her tail as Finley walks into the room.

"That's Lee, named after the great Liberace. His friends called him Lee, and Mr. Sparkle knew him as a friend. Also, Lee is for Jackie O's sister, Lee Radziwill."

Finley yawns and pets the dog. "Who's Liberace?"

"Oh, dear. Please don't let Chas hear you say that. He was the greatest classically trained pianist of the 20th century. And he did a lot for candelabras. Elton John copied his style, but Lee wore the capes and the jewels first. But enough about that. I'm Scott, Mr. Sparkle's better half. We have Danishes and coffee at Chez Sparkle, especially for a friend of Andrea's." He stands up and shakes Finley's hand.

"Elton John sings that song 'Rocket Man,'" Finley offers.

Scott stays silent and turns to his newspaper.

"Do you know what time Andrea will be back?" Finley sits down and reaches for a Danish.

"Usually, 8. After happy hour meetings and the Vegas rush hour." Scott turns the news page and crosses his legs.

"I could take a taxi later."

Each man chews in silence. Mr. Sparkle must be watching soap operas in his bedroom because *Days of Our Lives* can occasionally be heard over the white noise of air-conditioning.

Scott seems deep in thought, in a relaxed way; he just had his tan refined at the spa, and its caramel hue contrasts with his summer uniform of floral Hawaiian shirt with white slacks and a sports coat. "There's something I've been dying to ask you."

Finley freezes mid-Danish. Isn't he getting old for questions like, "What are your intentions toward my daughter?"

"Could you do Marshmallow, please?"

Finley swallows. "Marshmallow...doesn't get out of bed for less than $5,000, silly," he answers in the familiar falsetto, adding a bit of flouncy business with his hands.

Scott looks astonished...and laughs.

An Evening with Mr. Sparkle is underway the first Saturday after Thanksgiving. Finley volunteers as a stagehand to help with Andrea's anxieties. The event must exude festivity. Finley can hardly take his eyes off the red dress with its sequins barely covering his fiancée's generous figure or her Jimmy Choo feathered heels, but he knows she's much too busy for even a kiss.

The stage bursts with poinsettias and garlands. Mr. Glitz nutcrackers guard the scene, towering at seven feet tall. Finley notices Marshmallow depicted in a snowy woodland scene with other bunnies, and he almost feels part of the Sparkle, Inc. family. After hours of soundchecks and orchestra warm-ups, Finley starts checking his watch with a yawn. A cheery woman with red hair begins fine-tuning the chorus. Finley sits in a theater chair to listen to the music.

An acne-ridden teenager in a button-down shirt approaches him. He opens a green folder before tapping Finley on the shoulder. "Did you check the snow machines? You've got to hurry. Curtain's in ten minutes."

Finley realizes he's left something out. "I'm sorry, Audley. I'll go make sure they're set to go." He heads over to the end of stage-right and notices an errant snow machine not angled at the ceiling. The snow machine wiggles by itself. Finley looks towards the curtain and sees a furry hand moving it. He has to blink to believe his eyes.

A man in an orangutan suit without its costume head balances on a nearby ladder, looking at Finley with glazed eyes.

Finley notices a few drops of the machine's fluid leaking. "Be careful up there!"

The guy in the suit wobbles a bit and the ladder shakes. He steps down, missing a rung and falls.

He lies in a heap for a few seconds before Finley touches his shoulder. "Are you okay?

"Don't touch me! Get off me. Don't freaking touch me." The heavy man in the costume wobbles to his feet. "It's your problem now, dude, not my kind of snow fluid anyway," he says as he rushes down a hallway.

Finley wants to follow the guy, but he decides to fix the machine. He runs to stage-left to find the other snow machine ready to go. He hears a cellist in the auditorium. It's show time. Finley prepares to watch his first Mr. Sparkle show backstage; he functions as an unofficial assistant to the stage manager but, at the moment, he's enjoying the show along with the fans.

Scott begins playing a medley of jazzy holiday songs, but soon the MC announces Mr. Sparkle.

Incredibly, Chas seems two decades younger in the deep garnet tuxedo with the sequined bowtie. Mr. Sparkle waits for the applause to die down before starting the show and seems to light up like a Christmas tree as he basks in the love of his fans. "Good evening, ladies and germs. Merry Christmas and hoppy holidays! You know, I may have started in the biz by drawing your favorite orangutan. Charles Schultz? I knew him when he was working for peanuts! But seriously, folks, I always knew, when I saw Liberace onstage as a young boy— the stage was my calling. So...let's sing. Scott, some accompaniment, please?"

Scott plays an intro familiar to millions of Judy Garland fans before it became a Christmas standard.

"Have yourself a sparkly little Christmas," Mr. Sparkle croons. The audience goes mad for it. A dancer plays it up onstage in the Mr. Glitz suit, hiding behind a Christmas tree and a menorah.

"Make the Yuletide...gay." Mr. Sparkle looks at the audience. Scott pauses the piano accompaniment, and everyone has a moment.

And then the familiar jazz tune that has become Mr. Glitz's leitmotif begins. The orangutan dances to it in a very red, sequined tuxedo.

"Welcome to *Mr. Sparkle's Holiday Evening*! Coming from beautiful Las Vegas, we'll be right back!" Mr. Sparkle, however, becomes aware that something's awry with the performance. Earlier, the dancer that occupied the orangutan costume not only missed marks but grabbed the stage curtains to keep balance after almost falling. The dancer must be under the influence of any number of substances and is perhaps dangerous.

Andrea reaches full panic mode, and damage control becomes her agenda. A reviewer from *Entertainment Weekly* and various influencers can clearly be seen in the second row. If Mr. Sparkle wants to keep the annual holiday show going at Laga Brutto, disasters must be avoided.

Finley, wishing to soothe his girlfriend and prove his usefulness, has an idea. "Oh my god, I think that's the same guy I saw messing with the snow machine earlier. He looked stoned. I'll replace him. I've watched the rehearsals. Any monkey can do it!"

"You'll have to get the suit from him first! He's picked up a letter-opener backstage, and he's refusing to leave until he gets double his paycheck!"

Entering quietly from stage-left, Finley can see the situation deteriorating. He must act. He remembers every pre-game speech in his brief junior high football career. The coach told him, "You're not precise. You're not the fastest guy on the team. But, my God, you can tackle!"

And he is going to tackle that orangutan.

Finley executes the tackle, but the large man in the orangutan suit shrugs him off and runs for the stage. He lurks near Scott's piano, but Finley has another idea. Being a decent singer, he hopes to make the antics "part of the show."

He grabs the mic off the stand and motions to Scott.

The piano pauses.

"If you're blue and you don't know where to go to, why don't you go where fashion fits?"

Scott, being quite familiar with the song, quickly adjusts for Finley's tempo and key.

"Putting on the Glitz!" Finley starts chasing that orangutan back. If he wants to be part of the show, why not use it? The audience seems interested. "Orangutans upon the levy, orange fur among the bevy, all misfits..." He points the mic at the orangutan.

"Putting on the Glitz!" he unexpectedly joins in.

Finley returns to the verse, "That's where each orangutan with fur goes, every jungle evening in tuxedoes, rubbing elbows."

"Come with me, and we'll attend the jubilee of crazy monkey fits…"

Finley tries to hand the mic back to the orangutan, but the character runs offstage. Finley shrugs to the audience and finishes, "Putting on the Glitz!"

Finley completes a run around the neighborhood and finds Andrea already home. He contemplates his Vegas future. The name Robbie Roberts kept coming into his mind lap after lap. He leans with his hands on his thighs and takes deep breaths to cool down before walking into the house. Finley kicks off his tennis shoes, peels his sweaty shirt and shorts from his soaked body. He hangs them on a towel bar in Andrea's pink en-suite bathroom to dry.

Andrea often complains about the smell of his laundry; he hopes drying his running clothes before dumping them in the hamper will keep the peace. The air-conditioner blasts as he opens the glass shower door. He tries to find his bar of soap behind Andrea's array of products. He gives up and uses a strange bodywash that smells of sandalwood.

He stops lathering his head when he hears the bathroom door open.

Andrea smiles as she slips off her bikini. She joins him. His muscles ache, but he is never too tired for Andrea. She's more interested in removing chlorine from her hair than showering with him, however, and he waits during three rounds of Andrea's haircare before he kisses her and leaves the bathroom.

He doesn't bother getting dressed after drying off; he hopes Andrea will hurry up and join him in bed. After a few minutes of white noise from the ceiling fan, he falls asleep.

Andrea nudges him awake with a few light kisses, and they finish what they started.

Finley catches his breath, and his thoughts return to the future. Finally, he broaches the topic with his girlfriend.

"I suppose I owe you one for getting that orangutan suit back and saving the show," Andrea responds.

"You don't. But I do have an old score to settle."

"What do you mean?"

"Dad went on *Robbie Roberts Tonight!* with Marshmallow before he died, and Robbie Roberts kind of rattled him. I don't really know what he was getting at with the dirty questions about Marshmallow. I don't think Dad enjoyed it at all."

Andrea turns towards him on the satin sheets, squeezing her eyebrows upwards in thought. "Sparkle, Inc. has a pretty good relationship with Robbie Roberts, although he is obnoxious, but who isn't? You're not planning anything mean, are you? I can probably get you on the show, but what do you mean 'settle the score'? He just got out of rehab, and nobody wants him to start again on the cocaine."

Finley softens his tone. "I just think Marshmallow deserves a better interview, don't you?"

"Well, publicity wouldn't hurt. Can you mention Mr. Sparkle?"

"Of course."

ROBBIE ROBERTS TONIGHT!

The color gray is king on *Robbie Roberts Tonight!* The set has been updated over the decades but remains monochromatic. The Art Deco glass behind the plush seating brings a hint of the Chrysler Building to Las Vegas. *Robbie Roberts Tonight!* has never quite gone national, but some local cable channel always picks up the show. Maybe it's Robbie's smooth baritone voice or his slicked-back hair that defines his appeal. Even his deep-set brown eyes add a trustworthy look to a pleasant, if not handsome, face. Yet, he worries his charms are fading like his ratings.

The man, criticized for his youth when he'd started in the '90s, began aging like the rest of his generation. Openly loathing the blandness of his contemporaries, hosts like Carson Daly or Ryan Seacrest, he brings an edge of derision to every interview. His guests know full well he's going to lightly toast them if they don't stay on their toes. And he's worn a black double-breasted suit since 1998 in honor of John Larroquette's character, Dan Fielding. He's put on his lucky suit in preparation for a troublesome guest.

Nothing much has changed in the twenty-year-old format except his bandleader, Gouda. He calls Gouda's genre "sleazy listening." Everybody needs a gimmick in this town, and the ratings had gone up a bit.

He winces at the day's schedule, dreading his talk with that awful bunny. He'd been a bit high when he interviewed Kevin Luker years ago and had been downright mean. No one expected the man to die from the goddamn flu the following

Tuesday, for Christ's sake. But the bunny is always mean and grating, no matter whose hand is up her ass. He regards Finley as a lesser talent, riding the coattails of nepotism: the weaker of the two Marshmallow bunnies.

"They're out of my lemon loaf in the green room! Sons of bitches!" He shouts to no one in particular down the hall, "Sons of bitches!"

He turns towards the dressing room mirror, checking his tan and making sure his salt-and-pepper hair stays slicked. His stylist has been furloughed due to budget cuts, and he's questioning the decision. The redness of his eyes and inflammation around his nose worry him, but he hasn't lost his looks to drugs...yet. He walks a tight rope between cocaine and vanity in front of the camera, knowing his age is starting to show.

He still does one line of coke if his morning coffee doesn't hit him fast enough. Nobody's perfect, but he's already had his line this morning. It's not working, and he debates having another cup of coffee.

Robbie prays the coke works its magic as he sits in a tufted leather chair that he bought in midtown with his first paycheck. Gouda arrives in Robbie's dressing room, wearing a velvet cheetah-print suit, which clashes with Robbie's tasteful, masculine décor. Gouda always doublechecks his song list, not that Robbie cares; the band could play "Hava Nagila" repetitively, and he'd still put it on the air.

Finley knocks at the door instead of waiting in the green room. Gouda lifts an eyebrow. Even Robbie doesn't know what goes on behind the scenes of Gouda's head. The weathered man, Korean by way of Queens, must have a hell of a backstory to churn out all those offensive songs.

Gouda goes backstage with his signature politeness to rejoin The Stuffed Hams. Robbie turns to Finley and struggles to ask him to leave. "Mr. Luker. How nice to see you. Was the green room not to your liking? I'm very busy, but we can talk later."

"I think this room is a bit more comfortable," Finley says, deliberately ignoring all social cues. He seats himself in a predictable gray loveseat across from Robbie's chair. "What's in the decanter? I'm parched. What's the deal with all this gray? Did you accidentally hire a mortician instead of a decorator?"

Robbie lobs back, his energy returning, "It might seem that way to a guy who grew up on a puppet show—"

"—And the mad puppeteer who raised me had more talent than you can imagine." Finley takes a sip of whiskey.

"I had nothing against your father. I wanted him on the show, didn't I? Maybe it didn't land so well. The whole thing is ancient history. We lost a great man when he died, and maybe this is just sawdust, but you have my condolences."

Finley stands; his face softens a bit. "I guess that's my cue to go rehearse with Marshmallow. She's quite the diva these days." He doesn't look back to see Robbie's reaction, as if walking away from an explosion.

Terror. As his anger towards the talk show host dissipates, the butterflies ravage his stomach with lead boots. His father bombed hard in front of a live studio audience, and so had Marshmallow. Finley might be about to go down with the family ship.

Marshmallow seems to call out, "What about ME?" And Finley suddenly relaxes. This isn't reality; it's "magic theater." He just has to grab that feather and fly, right?

He catches the tail end of the chat with Kitty Foyle, a pop star who never would have appeared on the show a few years ago while trending. Roberts is really out of line, asking her about her breakup with a vile British comedian. Finley can almost see a tear forming in her lustrous eye, and his rage returns.

Robbie introduces him, and Marshmallow's song plays in an obnoxious rearrangement composed by The Stuffed Hams. He hugs Kitty (she looks like she needs it), and she clings before scooting down the gray couch.

"Whoa, get a room, you two!" Robbie leans over his enormous desk.

"I respect Kitty, but I happen to be engaged," Finley says in an even tone.

"And who's the lucky lady?"

"Andrea Rizzo."

"Congratulations! Did having famous fathers bring you two together? Just to let our audience know, Andrea is the daughter of Mr. Sparkle, and Finley's father was the late, great Kevin Luker, creator of *The Marshmallow Show*."

"You can say that. Really, I took one look and fell in love," Finley replies.

"And I hear you've also brought another special lady here, Marshmallow herself! Can you talk a little bit about the show's history before we meet her?"

Finley clears his throat. "My father ran the entire communications wing at Vanderbilt in the '80s. He was a DJ before that. He created the Marshmallow character to pester my aunt when they were kids. He started the show with some students from the university's TV department. An executive at Nickelodeon saw it one day, and the rest is history."

"Does anyone ever compare you to your father?" Robbie leans forward a bit while asking.

"Oh, all the time. It's like a thorn in my side, kind of like Marshmallow herself, really. But, you know, I can't live with her, and I can't live without her. Her grating voice is ingrained in my soul. Sometimes, I just wanted to strangle her in her sleep because she had her own room in our house when I was a kid. But...puppets never sleep." He says this in deadpan fashion, but the audience gasps, and then they laugh.

"I'd like to hear Marshmallow's side of the story," Robbie says flatly.

She begins, "Finley is a textbook case of neurotic jealousy. He knew I was the favorite, and he couldn't deal with it. Not all of us can sparkle and shine in this bunny business!"

"Well." Robbie Roberts conspiratorially leans towards Marshmallow. "I'd say Finley is on his way to either one of two places: a comeback tour or therapy."

"I guess he can tag along on MY comeback tour!" Marshmallow huffs in her diva voice.

"I'd love to see that, and I hope you'll keep Las Vegas in mind!"

With that, the bit concludes, and Finley moves over for the next guest, another former wrestler in an action movie. Kitty helps him get the hang of repetitive clapping and smiling; somehow, he feels less alone. He's landed on his feet, and Robbie actually helped him get there. Maybe the talk show host isn't such a bad guy all the time. He relaxes as he hears the familiar strains of the *Robbie Roberts Tonight!* theme, and Gouda finishes the show with a trumpet solo.

A letter engraved on ecru monogrammed stationery with the curved initials **RR** travels through the Vegas postal system and lands at Mr. Sparkle's sprawling Mediterranean ranch house. Finley has taken up residence over the past six months, sharing Andrea's bedroom. The letter marks the first correspondence Finley receives as a member of that household that's not a bill or junk mail. He doesn't open it at first, so it sits on the credenza that holds all incoming mail until Andrea or the house maid sorts envelopes.

After a few minutes, at the dining table, Finley realizes the letter contains the only reasonable offer of gainful employment he has received in years:

Finley,

That bit we did went down pretty well, didn't it? You made your old man proud. How would you and Marshmallow like a recurring role on the show? Even Gouda came around to the idea and that's rare. Your act could be like the ugly Rottweiler puppet on that other show, but I guess Marshmallow doesn't smoke cigars.

Don't call me, I'll call you.

RR

"Recurring" has a magic ring to Finley. His career hasn't died so much as faded; he can now carry on the family legacy with creative control over a formerly hated sibling, a vengeance impossibly sweet. As a college dropout with a string of failed romances before Andrea's surprising attentions, Finely somehow has won at love and had it been lucky for his professional life. He ought to send a thank you card to the drunken dancer he tackled.

Marshmallow's first appearances on the show had been as light and vapid as the namesake confection. He could almost see a glint of creative differences in her glass eyes, but a puppet has little say in the matter. Today, rather hot for April, Finley strolls into Robbie's unlocked office at The Silver Rush Casino. There's silence which concerns him. Something seems wrong, very wrong. He looks around the office and sees a gray bit of clothing behind the desk. Finley walks around for a moment before he sees Robbie Roberts.

Robbie lies face-down in a heap, slowly breathing. Has he had a stroke or a heart attack? There is nothing nearby but a giant carton of Tropicana with a straw sticking out of it, but it smells much more like whiskey and something unidentifiable than it does of citrus.

Finley quickly calls 911 from his cell phone and sits on the leopard-print loveseat, a gift from Gouda, no doubt. He can hear the large office clock above him ticking out the minutes. It seems like an eternity before two young paramedics arrive.

Finley leaves the office to give them room. He walks into the bathroom and splashes water on his face. He hears the paramedics loading Robbie onto a gurney, and asks, "Where are you taking him? Can I ride in the ambulance?"

"He's going to Dignity Health. They might put him in the psych ward after they pump his stomach. You can't ride unless you're a close relative," the younger paramedic answers in a calm voice.

Finley watches as Robbie leaves the building. After getting directions upstairs, Finley gets in his Mustang and drives. Hours at Dignity Health follow. After a terrible cup of coffee, he notices that the fluorescent lights flicker every few minutes.

A tired, startlingly young physician gives the group in the waiting room an update. All the while, he stares quite a bit at Gouda. He must be unfamiliar with *Robbie Roberts Tonight!* "Physically, he's going to make it. I'm still not sure what was in the orange juice, but the lab is working on it. He's going to be unconscious for a couple days, and I'm recommending that he wakes up in our psychiatric unit."

Finley winces at Robbie's predicament. Robbie's not going to like waking up in the psychiatric unit one bit. This was no suicide attempt: it was an addict possibly trying to find a "healthier" alternative to cocaine, adding Vitamin C even, Finley theorizes. Unfortunately, Robbie's amateur chemistry skills are even shittier than his aptitude for self-care. "Do you think he was making some concoction to sub in for coke?" Finley whispers to Gouda.

"I don't know. He has been listening to The Suicide Albums a lot lately," Gouda says in a sad manner.

Shocked, Finley asks, "You mean like Slipknot or something?"

Gouda shakes his head. "No, I mean the albums Frank Sinatra recorded after Ava left him during the filming of *Mogambo*. You know, 'The Wee Small Hours,' 'Only the Lonely,' 'When No One Cares'? The lights really went out in Vegas back then. You can't get much darker, man." Gouda pauses, clears his throat, still conspiratorially whispering, "How would you feel about being a guest-host?"

Finley doesn't answer at first, and the sounds of a doctor's shoes squeaking down the polished linoleum become almost deafening. After raising an eyebrow, he ultimately accepts. The show must go on—even an unconscious Robbie Roberts would agree.

Blinking after he removes his sunglasses, the endless hotel-casino blasts him with its air-conditioning. Didn't Beck use to sing about an "air-conditioned sun?" Finley knows what that means now. Walking a bit on the busy low-pile carpet to a restaurant, but unsure which option would be best for nursing a hangover headache, he notices a familiar figure at a slot machine.

Robbie isn't close to winning a jackpot, and Finley can tell his presence is being deliberately ignored. He loudly clears his throat and asks, "Aren't you supposed to be in the hospital?"

Robbie doesn't look up from the slot machine. "That doctor's a real quack, but we got an understanding. And you're not guest-hosting the show yet. *Recurring*, Finley, you're a recurring guest!"

Two cherries and a lemon pop up on the tackiest Carmen Miranda-themed slot Finley has ever seen. It's a tropical nightmare that would make even the carpet on the ceiling in Elvis's old Jungle Room blush.

"Sons of bitches!" Robbie slaps the slot machine with an open palm. "Where are we eating?" Robbie stands up in a gray suit with a sharkskin sheen. He's finally done playing the slot, and Finley is at least relieved he isn't eating alone. The overdose isn't a topic he can bring up now.

Later, Finley notices Robbie's hands are shaking while he holds a menu.

Coming back from the men's room, Finley sees a guy sitting in his seat, across from Robbie. He's wearing sunglasses and whispering with the talk show host. He has some sort of accent. Australian? Finley sits next to Robbie and rescues his root beer from the Australian. He reads the dessert menu a few times, hoping the waiter will return. He gives another look across the table. He now recognizes the movie star. Finley exclaims, "You're The Puma! I love that movie!"

The Australian takes off his sunglasses. "This is exactly why I'm in Vegas. You see, Finn, I don't want to be 'The Puma' anymore. I'm John Tuckman, first and foremost. The movie didn't do well critically, but people still think of me as The Puma. I don't have a magic belt or a sidekick. I can't really fly. Did you know I graduated from L'atelier de Sens in Paris and started as a chef? I was catering the movie when the original actor got sick, and the director asked me to audition. The rest, you see, is history. But good old Robbie here, he can make things right as rain again. We're discussing having a food segment on the show." Tuckman bites into a slice of Canadian bacon.

After slicing up his pancake, Robbie cuts into the conversation. He points a butter knife at Tuckman and says, "You'd be recurring, just like Finley. It's working pretty well for the guy's career. He's even auditioning for a film role."

Finley chimes in, "We certainly need better food on the set."

"Shrimp ceviche is my signature dish. Have you seen my show, *Down Under Edibles?*"

Finley nods, a white lie. What a name for a show!

The Aussie gives a firm handshake and exclaims, "Good on you. If you play your cards right, I might let you see the old Rolls Royce. Now, if you wouldn't mind, I'd like to talk privately with Robbie here."

Finley leaves a few twenties to cover his bill. He's not sure if Robbie or John look up to see him walk away, but he feels relief that at least Robbie won't be alone today.

Finley climbs the ladder out of the pool, wishing Chas's Fourth of July party was over. He can't do laps when so many Vegas denizens in bikinis sun themselves leathery brown on neon floats. The men in Speedos lounge on deck chairs or mill about with Mr. Sparkle's latest martini invention, The American Sparkler.

He towels off and has to sun-dry before he can play video games in the basement. He overhears Tuckman and Robbie arguing over food with Scott.

"You've got to sear any kind of protein. And season it first," Scott points out, as if trying to reason with Robbie and John.

"Steaks belong on the grill, never the frying pan," Robbie retorts.

"The barbie may be one way, but it's not the only chook in the coop. And I'm the top chef here," Tuckman fumes.

"This is The Fourth of July! The great American charcoal grill is the George Washington of food preparation, and you're a bunch of asshole Benedict Arnolds." Robbie leaves the other two on that note, stalking off to get more Korean barbecue skewers.

Scott turns over on his stomach to sun his other side, and Tuckman guzzles a sparkling water from a red glass.

Finley decides to walk over to the Aussie. "How's it going?"

"I'm calling him Robbie Rotten from now on, that's how it's going," Tuckman replies.

Finley stands there, moving the umbrella in his drink from side to side. Maybe the only company anyone needs on

July 4th is time with the Mario Brothers. "I don't know what to say."

"Why don't you get a refill then? I'll work on my tan." Tuckman takes off his sunglasses and closes his eyes. His striped chaise lounge gleams beside a palm tree; it sits upon bleached-white concrete.

Finley, putting on an unbuttoned Key lime-patterned shirt and Hawaiian swim trunks, begins making his way out of the pool area, dodging conversations. He overhears his name in a hushed conversation between two bikini-clad women, a brunette in gold and a redhead in green. He adjusts his sunglasses and stretches out on a lounge chair nearby.

"He's living here with her," the brunette whispers.

"What does he do for a living?" The redhead sips a wine cooler, only half-interested in Andrea's love life.

The brunette whispers, although still audible to Finley. "He's an actor. You know Andrea bought the rights to *The Marshmallow Show*? Well, she's getting benefits. Finley was set to take over as Marshmallow. But she cancelled it. He's still living here. In Andrea's room."

"Is he hot?" The redhead yawns, applying sunscreen around her belly button. Then she wiggles her toes, painted raspberry blue.

"He's hot. Mama likes," the brunette finishes, licking her upper lip.

"Maybe I should go into television myself."

They both return to their tans, midriffs exposed and glistening with oil.

Finley gets up; it's one thing to be called handsome, but he has a job now. He's recurring on *Robbie Roberts Tonight!*, isn't he? A man has his pride. He's not just Andrea's boytoy. He sees Andrea engaged in conversation near the lawn, sipping on wine and throwing her head back in laughter. Finley realizes he's tired of the party and the crowd of strangers.

He heads back past the pool, goes inside and into the room he shares with Andrea. He walks to the closet across vacuumed high-pile, beige carpet; his footsteps become inaudible, and the quiet of the room helps him forget the party. The constant whir of air-conditioning makes a soothing noise. He opens Marshmallow's box and sits on the bed with the puppet. He starts by moving her head, and as she becomes more animated, he gives voice to the puppet.

"Didn't we tell you? You have to sparkle and shine at a party!" She clasps her hands and sways at his direction.

"I'm not feeling festive, Marshmallow. And I don't want steak or burgers or hot dogs or fireworks," he says in a downcast sort of way.

"Everyone has their own ways of celebrating holidays. Every bunny, big and small, has a party in the bunny hall," she recites.

Finley frowns at the bunny and says, "That was from episode six. Why do you always rhyme and make terrible puns?"

"That's how I sparkle and shine, silly!" The puppet claps her hands for emphasis.

"Finley!"

He turns to see Andrea standing at the door.

"Where did you go? The guests went home. I wanted to introduce you to my friends." She pouts, then stares at Marshmallow. "What the hell?"

"Sometimes...doing a ventriloquist routine is comforting. I can throw my voice, you know? I've been doing it my whole life," he says without looking at her.

"You need comforting? It's the Fourth of July! Jesus Christ!" She paces in front of him, folding her arms.

"I heard your friends talking about me. They said... They said you just wanted sex. They said I didn't have a job." He exhales after letting it out.

She sits down on the bed, stroking his leg. "I do want you. Is that so bad?" She kisses him then says, "Everything's fine. You don't need that damn bunny."

"Everything's fine." He throws Marshmallow in the box and locks the door.

Even with the threat of rehab and cancellation hanging over his head, Robbie heads over to see the only doctor he needs, Dr. Petrov. Maybe she can alter the dozens of prescriptions to help him wean off cocaine and alcohol. She's done it before, right?

Dr. Petrov's office lies in the basement level of a somewhat defunct mini-mall on the outskirts of the Vegas Strip. Operating on the edges of legality, the doctor doesn't want to be found by just anyone, operating on word-of-mouth. She's not even in the *Yellow Pages*. He's not sure Olga Petrov is her real name.

The receptionist stands outside on the cracked concrete, smoking. Olga's son greets Robbie with a nod, and his pinched face almost smiles. Robbie signs himself in and knocks five times on Olga's door. The fluorescent lights seem louder than usual and the torn linoleum even more decrepit. Olga nods him in, and he follows her down an impossibly long hallway. The office at the end gleams like an oasis of luxury compared to the deliberate squalor of the waiting room. He can't stop looking at the cascade of blonde flowing around her beautiful face or the light blue dress that's tight in all the right places.

"What a week I've had! Thanks for getting me out of Dignity Health." He kisses her angled cheek.

"No more overdoses." She puffs a cigarette and taps it against a sculptural ash tray. "It's okay to be an addict but don't go too far."

Robbie looks at the ground. "I guess it's over between us. You know I have HIV."

"I do, too."

"What?! Did you give it to me?"

"I think it might be the other way around." She caresses his thigh.

He pauses and adds, "Do you want to get a room then?"

"Let me tell Yuri I'm taking off, okay? The usual at The Realm of Venus?"

"Olga...you save me. Hit me? I can't cold turkey."

She kisses him and hands him an envelope.

"Welcome to *John Tuckman's Australian Kitchen*. I'd like to thank the sponsors and old Robbie here for the new digs. Today, I'll be making a stuffed ham. But I'd like to talk to you about cheese for a moment. The Australian is a cheese connoisseur. American cheese and Velveeta can go right where they belong: in the rubbish, ladies and gentlemen. That stuff isn't cheese. And don't get Australians started on what you call coffee. So, if you're watching at home, throw your Folgers in the rubbish, right along with the Velveeta. Now, you're thinking in Australian!

"If you're like most Australians, you might wonder, what am I going to do with the leftover Christmas ham? I know you might be eating turkeys here in the States, but we don't have those in Australia. Father Christmas is on his way, so you'll need this recipe in your Christmas future. Or you might need it for some Thanksgiving ham. This really is a cross between a good old ham sanga, that's what you'd call a sandwich, and what you'd call French toast, but we Aussies call it a puff."

Tuckman puts on an Australian flag apron and shows the live audience the ingredients. His bright white shirt shows off his tan, muscled physique. He puts the ham casserole in the studio oven with Aussie flourish and turns to Camera 1 with a toothsome grin.

"While we wait on our stuffed ham to finish cooking, here's a song from Gouda and The Stuffed Hams!"

Gouda, clad in a white T-shirt, pointy crocodile shoes, skinny black tie, and zebra-print leather pants, nods to his drummer to begin the percussion for a spoken word opening.

"Zig-da-da-zig-a-be-da-be-be
If you cook the ham 'til it's overdone
If you fry the spam for everyone
If you cut the can in the frying pan
If you move your feet, then it's time for ham.
Jazz is more than rock and roll:
It's beatnik shoes with a rubber sole."

Gouda reaches for his trumpet and plays a few bars of "How High the Moon" as a segue to commercial break.

Tuckman moves in for his closeup. "We'll be right back with the finished ham casserole. Remember, like the song says, how high the moon? We'll find out how high the sandwich when we come back." He holds his smile, and the cameraman says, "Cut!"

Tuckman's smile fades and he rearranges a bell pepper rose on an ornate platter. He asks, "Did you get a closeup of the casserole?'

"Yes. We got it from multiple angles."

"Presentation can never be too perfect, you know?" Tuckman warns him.

Robbie comes out of his office. He walks across the stage and steals a shrimp from the platter, savors it. "And it tastes great, too."

"Let me finish the scene before you eat the meal, please." Tuckman stares at Robbie with exasperation.

"G'day mate! I'm John Tuckman! Put a shrimp on the barbie! But don't grill me kangaroo!" Finley's proud of his Tuckman impression and shares it with Andrea over Chinese takeout.

"The Australian on the show is John Tuckman?" Andrea says the Australian's name with a kind of dread.

"Yes. He's doing cooking segments on the show."

"Oh." She examines the noodles on her fork.

"Do you hate his food or something?"

"We dated a while. He dumped me right before Valentine's Day. I bought a goddamn pink Versace gown, too!" A tear threatens to make its way out of the corner of her eye.

"Wear it for me." Finley leans in to kiss her cheek. He's careful to check his jealousy.

Finley stands in white shorts, part of a tennis outfit Andrea picked out for him. The estate includes a modest indoor tennis court; why not utilize it? He swings the racket a bit in practice and feels the whoosh. He's mastered ping pong, but rarely has he played tennis. His precision in ping pong varies between intermediate and flashes of brilliance, but maybe he'll have better luck here. Andrea has the idea that playing doubles with her fathers will help Finley know them better.

Mr. Sparkle, wearing green, comes out with a handkerchief to wipe his brow. Scott walks beside his husband with deep strides, gripping his racket with shades of athleticism. He plans to win and sees little competition on his home court.

Andrea glides onto the tennis court, and Finley can't take his eyes off the curves stressed by her tennis dress. He catches a designer logo emblazoned on the skirt, gleaming white, and the same logo on white suede sneakers. Her charm bracelet tinkles as she sets up a practice serve. She pulls off looking glamorous and athletic. Full makeup and a high ponytail finish the look. "Finley, you and Scott versus me and Dad." Andrea points her racket to the other side of the net. She takes her place beside her father. She leans forward and bends her knees as if the game has already started.

"Let me apologize in advance for your imminent crushing defeat," Scott says with a grin.

"Let Dad serve first then, if you're so sure of yourself," Andrea retorts, pointing the tennis racket at Scott.

Mr. Sparkle nods and wipes off invisible perspiration with one of his sporty ascots. He serves underhand and Finley manages to lob it back. Scott sends the ball flying, but Andrea barely misses with a savage swing that fails to connect. They start up another volley that lasts an impressive ten minutes.

Mr. Sparkle, however, calls a timeout, short of breath and wheezing a bit. He sits nearby on an astonishing piece of furniture: a glamorous, light blue deck chair that longs to become a chaise lounge with its overstuffed cushions. He lets Andrea take over their side of the net. But Andrea can't cover every shot by herself.

Finally, Chas calls out, "I guess we have to forfeit this match."

Lee, the beagle, prances onto the tennis court as if to lend moral support to Mr. Sparkle. She sits on her blue velvet cushion that matches her owner's deck chair. She wags her tail and licks Mr. Sparkle's cheek as he leans over to pet her.

Buoyed by this demonstration, Chas stands up and swooshes his racket with renewed vigor. "I'm back in the game." He takes his place by his daughter.

But Scott and Finley stay in the lead. Lee gets more vocal with barking and chases the tennis ball, so the group decides to call it day.

Finley and Scott's team have won the first tennis match.

"You played well, Finley. Very sporting, old bean." Mr. Sparkle uses a mock British accent and shakes Finley's hand over the net.

"It's not about the game. It's about bonding with Andrea's family." Finley looks over to his girlfriend with worshipful eyes.

They walk off together and Lee barks after them.

FIDELITY

We have come to the casinos
To stop the endless clink of coin
We are searching for our brothers,
Oh, Cubans, will you join?

Faithful to my people
To stop the endless flow
Of monies from ill-gotten gain
And mustached criminals!
I, Fidel, will lead you
Like a river of generosity!

Falling in love with another person transforms the patterns of life. Finley feels wonder throughout the entire process, certain that Andrea will change her mind. Youth, symmetry of features, and general good health sometimes combine to create that most fragile thing: happiness. The kind of happiness the aged might remember for solace.

Mr. Sparkle's sprawling estate includes a swimming pool, and Finley loves to swim in it. Surrounded by palm trees and succulents, the pool appears to be a desert oasis complete with a monogrammed "S" for Sparkle spelled out on the pool's concrete side.

Since Andrea has been hearing wedding bells, she's started dieting with cottage cheese and grapefruit, just like Jacqueline Kennedy Onassis (or so she says). Finley hopes swimming laps will be enough for him to look perfect in the Dolce and Gabbana tuxedo he knows Andrea fantasizes about because he doesn't want to give up cheese Danishes. He worries while alternating between the breaststroke and the crawl if his salary from *Robbie Roberts Tonight!* will even begin to cover rings for Andrea or the lavish honeymoon she envisions. Rome or Tahiti, she often tells him; maybe both.

The blue, chlorinated water carries him lap after lap, from one end to the other. His frustrations cause him to dig faster into the water and quicken his flipper kick. He could start auditioning, talk to his father's old agent and leave another message. He'd taken acting classes in college. He has some momentum from the talk show going, doesn't he? He has some looks going for him, or at least that's what Andrea tells him. He could play the zany best friend in something, perhaps? He's suddenly out of breath in the middle of the pool and turns over to finish the lap with a backstroke.

"You've got a voicemail, Finley," Scott mentions as Finley walks in through the sliding door.

He thinks Glenda would have left a message on his cell phone, not the house phone. Toweling off his wet hair, Finley listens to that familiar voice.

"Finley, nice to hear from you! So sorry about your father. One of the greats. Actually, there is a movie role available. It's a biopic about Fidel Castro. You'll have to audition for it though."

He calls Glenda right back on the house phone, "Hello?"

"Hello? Finley! I'm glad I got a hold of you. How do you feel about the movie?"

Fidel Castro? Anything's worth a shot. "I'm… interested."

"Wonderful! I've got the ball rolling. The producers have agreed to hold the audition at your place. I think they might want a tour of the Sparkle house. Anyway, you'll feel more comfortable that way. I know it's been a while since your last audition. I can get you a copy of the script, but they're revising it."

"Do you know who's directing it?" Finley plays with the telephone cord.

"Well, his name is Provocateur. He's kind of a fresh face, but his first film got some attention at the festivals. He's very unconventional, but I think this could be a great learning experience for you. As an actor."

"Uh-oh. What are you not telling me?"

"He's sort of inexplicable, mysterious. You'll just have to meet him. I'll get the script to you as soon as possible, but just focus on the first 15 pages. You don't have to be off book yet; they'll let you have the script at the table reading."

"Did they give you a date and time for this audition?"

"Tomorrow afternoon at 1:00. I think one of the producers plans to fly back to Santiago, so time is of the essence. Be ready earlier, though. In this business, being on time means being ready 15 minutes early."

"Okay... Can you get me the script today? Maybe fax it to me?"

"Sure thing. And Good luck, Finley."

The next day, five producers and the director arrive a few minutes early. Finley shows them around to the best of his ability and leads them to the mirrored dining room table. He assumes the youngest man in the group—the one with long black hair, a red beret, and black nail polish on his left hand—must be Provocateur. He says little but indicates with a gesture to Finley that the reading should begin.

"Flies! Heat! They are no match for the Revolutionary! We will crush the corruption of gambling, the sick stench of Batista, and the mafia's choking fingers around Cuba's neck forever. It is I, Fidel, who orders it so!" Finley reads these lines with passion in an accent that sounds a bit more French than Cuban. He'd taken more French than Spanish in school, and he's aware it could be showing. He's not sure what reaction he's getting from the quiet group seated at the dining table. They greet Mr. Sparkle's lavish home with apparent distaste, but a sweaty man named George Pinkman at least accepted Finley's offer of coffee and a Danish. The afternoon light shows off the stained-glass Baroque cherubs in the dining room window to full effect, but Finley doubts their magic is working today.

Finally, the small woman named Judith with the squirrel-like face speaks. She glances at a few of her cohorts. They seem to have reached an agreement. The balding man next to George in the blue button-down whispers something in Judith's ear. Another producer named Jorge wipes off his glasses with his shirt sleeve and takes a hard look at Finley's features. "How would you feel about wearing a fake nose?" She stares at his nose as if it's the only thing in the world.

"I would do it...for Fidel," he answers. Although he's not a Communist, he does want the role. He sees Provocateur whisper something else into Judith's ears, and she nods.

A decision has been made.

"I think I speak for all of us. We've found our Castro!" She looks around the table, and everyone nods. "We expect principle photography to begin in June. Our scriptwriters should fly in from Cuba around that time. We're very close to finding our Che Guevara and our Batista. We're very much looking forward to filming *Fidelity*. Welcome to the team!"

They all shake hands, but Provocateur clicks the heels of his boots in a snap and bows dramatically. The director's bright blue eyes seem unreadable, and Finley doesn't quite know if the man is pleased with the audition.

Finley shuts the door then buries himself in the most ridiculous script he's read in his life, but at least he won't be playing a bunny this time.

Andrea walks in a short time later and puts down her keys. "Who in the hell were those weirdos in my house?"

"I've just been hired to play Fidel Castro in an upcoming biopic," he says nonchalantly, still reading.

"Jesus Christ, Finley."

Some filming for *Fidelity* was inexplicably being done in Las Vegas. Finley thought the casino locations, trying to pass for 1940s Havana, were at least as convincing as the fake nose on his face.

Today, they were filming his first scene: Castro, enraged at mob corruption in Havana, smashes a slot machine in a hotel casino. When did this happen? Finley wonders, doing his best to get into character.

"Historical accuracy often plays second fiddle to dramatic license in biopics," the director assures.

Finley knows him only by his long hair, beard, and the name Provocateur.

The owners of The New Jersey, New Jersey Casino had not agreed to the destruction of a vintage machine, so

Provocateur negotiated a compromise. "Fidel" was to smash the least popular slot machine with a mallet, that one being called Emoji. During postproduction, a more authentic vintage machine could be created using CGI.

Finley struggles to become enraged with righteousness and recites his lines while harmlessly pounding the casino carpet. During the entire process, an elderly couple stares at him like he is deranged, and his fake nose wobbles with each pound of the mallet, but creativity is undeterred. "I destroy you, Moloch of Capitalism! We will never submit to the vile schemes of criminals. I will drive you from the land of Cuba with all your filthy coins! I liberate the proletariat from the crutch of entertainment!"

"Great energy, Finley! But don't lose the accent so much!" Provocateur eyes the actor's process with serenity. The film will surely make a statement. "Tomorrow, you will cast out the demons of Capitalism from the swine herd that overruns the casino floor."

"Is the management going to let you do that?" Finley stares at the carpet doubtfully.

"I'm afraid the herd will only consist of about three pigs, but we plan to make the most of them on screen."

"Do you think we're going too far with the whole 'Fidel is Christ' symbolism?"

"Fidel represents many things, but he is mostly a god of art. Cuba becomes a canvas, the Cuban people a sacrifice to his canvas. Fidel may be a real man but, in my view, he is a work of art. Fidel becomes art on a silver screen, and art is larger than life. And I am the director. I write in lightning with my finger and create the film. I am Provocateur! Go big or go home!" He stares at Finley, daring him to disagree.

"Okay, then, is there anything I need to know about working with pigs?"

"Feed them apples between takes."

After a long morning of hair and makeup, Finley digs into a cheese Danish. He's waiting for Provocateur to finish up with the actor playing Che Guevara. He should be worried about Che upstaging him because Provocateur has found a kindred spirit in a young Socialist actor named Jason. But he's grateful to have someone distract the talkative director. Finley thinks the prodigious amount of marijuana Jason smokes minimizes any sort of Socialist intensity on set. He starts to worry the film is becoming an unintended comedy.

"Scene! Quiet on the set!" Provocateur sits to watch the actors in knee-high boots and a red beret. "Finley, Fidel is exhausted from swimming away from the Batistas through shark-infested waters. Che is tending to his arm that has been scraped by a passing shark's skin."

Finley nods and sees Jason's glazed, half-lidded eyes focusing on the floor.

Jason vaguely nods after almost a minute. "Fidel, your arm! Let me look at it."

"There are men in camp that require medical attention far more greatly. History will absolve me, but not the shark that attempted to aid the Capitalist pigs! We must strike in Havana soon!"

"Yes, Fidel! How I hate the tourists flooding in our great city while our poor people suffer under the weight of American oppression."

"I, Fidel, agree."

Exhausted after a day of destroying a slot machine, Finley orders a drink, still in costume, complete with an unconvincing spray-tan meant to make him look more like Castro. At least the guayabera and olive drab khakis are comfortable, although the military boots are less so.

The petite brunette bartender eyes him with amusement before approaching him. "And who are you supposed to be?"

"Fidel Castro."

"Really! What would Castro like to drink?"

"Cuba libre—lime, rum, and Coca-Cola?"

"I'll see what I can do, comrade."

Despite Provocateur's moral indignation regarding Capitalism, he proves to be a game drinking buddy for Finley after many long day shoots. The unlikely duo gets plenty of stares from the bar patrons after Provocateur arrives fashionably late. Although a shoot in Miami was originally planned, the production seems destined to remain in Las Vegas and California for convenience.

"We're going to film in the Dominican Republic to add authenticity to the jungle scenes. Just for a few weeks. I'll let you know the schedule," Provocateur says after ordering a similar drink.

Finley nods; he stares into the air as the waitress hands the director his order.

"I'm picturing a dream sequence for Fidel," Provocateur says after a silence spent gazing into an unprovocative rum and Coke.

Finley's eyes land on Provocateur's black nail-polished fingers tightly gripping the highball glass.

"Now is your opportunity to join me in the creative process, Finley. Creative synthesis becomes art. Art fuels dreams. Think of Fidel. Of what, does Fidel dream?"

"Percussion of marching boots... Revolution?"

"It's too drab for film! There's too much khaki in it already. Maybe we can focus on nightmarish hotel casinos with colorful dancers, and then you could bust up more slot machines? We should make use of the Vegas location."

"I'm pretty good with a mallet, my friend," Finley says in his "Fidel voice," which hasn't gotten much better since his audition. Finley knows he is possibly miscast and participating in a project that will never win much acclaim, but he feels a sense of accomplishment acting without Marshmallow or Sparkle, Inc..

He may be dating out of his league, but hopefully Andrea will come around to the finished film. The independent film is set to premiere in Vegas, fall 2004.

Oversleeping one lazy day back at Chez Sparkle's after filming wrapped in August, Finley walks over to join everyone at breakfast. Scott and Mr. Sparkle seem deep in conversation, eying him with pent-up excitement.

"Do you know you've gotten a package this morning?" Scott asks.

"From who?"

"My God, it's from Jack Palance!"

"The guy from *City Slickers?*"

"And several other films! He's a living legend. We're dying for you to see what's in there." Scott seems ready to burst at the seams of his Hawaiian shirt.

Finley can see that he won't be able to eat a cheese Danish or drink his coffee until he opens the mystery box. Inside the parcel is a professionally wrapped red present. He finally uncovers a wooden box and a handwritten note. He reads it aloud to an enthralled audience. "*From one Fidel to another. Have some smokes on me! - Jack.*"

"Cuban cigars! Did Palance ever play Fidel Castro?" Finley asks.

"I think so," Mr. Sparkle says slowly. "Omar Sharif played Che Guevara in it, too. Never saw the movie, though. There shouldn't be that much olive drab on the silver screen, in my opinion. Castro may have had some political savvy, but he gets zero stars for fashion sense."

"I don't think that's what he was aiming at." Finley feels a rush of pride at being recognized for his role in the movie.

An exhausted Finley returns to what he has nicknamed Sparkle House, only to find a guest waiting for him. Robbie has obviously been helping himself to the whiskey from the decanter in the living room and pensively sits in the most comfortable chair. "I've never seen you without a sports coat," Finley says, noting Robbie's surprising thinness without the perennial shoulder padding.

"Buffoonery." Robbie eyes the Fidel nose and guayabera shirt with derision.

"Salaried, artistic buffoonery, yes." Finley decides to join his guest and pours himself a whiskey. He has become less of a teetotaler these days. Must be the Vegas influence. "We see Castro as a symbol of Communism, everything reprehensible. But Castro saw America, gambling, and everything in Vegas as reprehensible. Too bad the film doesn't really say anything like that, but the show must go on."

"What about that Provocateur guy?" Robbie almost whispers, mulling over the film.

"He wishes to be a self-styled auteur," Finley tries to imbue the statement with some confidence.

"Oh, does he? He's a self-styled son of a bitch. You've got to have one successful movie to be an auteur." Robbie leans back, sipping the whiskey as if he's just made a winning chess move.

"*The Seagulls* won a prize at Cannes," Finley reminds.

"I heard that movie was...for the birds," Robbie cracks, but even he knows he's made a bad joke.

Finley sits on the armchair next to Robbie. "What are you really doing here, Robbie?"

The talk show host buries his face in his hands. "Gouda told me that the show is over if I overdose one more time. He'll go to the sponsors and our producer, and they'll cut ties with me. He's threatening to install you as a guest-host until he finds a replacement."

"Or he could get John Tuckman. But that hasn't happened yet. It's still your show. All you have to do is not overdose. What's the problem?"

"Did it ever occur to you or Gouda to ask why I would overdose? No. You're just like those asshole doctors, making life-changing decisions for me."

"Okay, you got me. I'm an asshole. Why did you overdose?"

"I'm HIV-positive."

Finley stays silent a moment, trying to find the right words. "I'm sorry to hear that...but as far as the show goes, everyone supports you. All you have to do is not overdose. Now, if you'll excuse me, this nose is itchy, and I need some sleep. I'm sure Mr. Sparkle won't mind if you use the guest room. You'll love the cheese Danishes at breakfast."

Robbie takes a swig of whiskey. "Asshole." But his tone isn't angry. He takes some loose pills out of a pants pocket, swallowing them down with more whiskey. He stands with determination.

"Oh my God, stop with the pills!" Finley stares in horror.

"Relax, it's just a supplement. I'm going to that guest room, you son of a bitch." He points upstairs with his cigar. "And I'm eating your Danish in the morning!"

"Fidel has no need for the confections of the bourgeoisie. Only the omelet of the proletariat!"

"Save it for the set. Your movie needs it." Robbie heads upstairs. "I'm gonna take a leak."

The filming in the Dominican Republic is grueling. Yet Finley's sober delivery of Fidel Castro's courtroom speech garners applause from the principal crew. "History will absolve me!" becomes a high point for Finley, almost making up for the terrors of the small plane ride to the island and the constant presence of mosquitoes.

One morning, Provocateur drives Finley to a dance studio. Finley walks amid a row of modest pastel houses and into a former warehouse. The well-lit interior belies the humble first impression, and a beautiful brunette in red introduces herself as the instructor. Provocateur sits nearby in a metal folding chair to oversee the lesson. Jason and an actress named Juana stretch to prepare for the class.

"Fidel doesn't dance," Finley protests to the director.

"At some point, he did. I want you to experience dance so that you can reject it. Rejecting the salsa to a Cuban in those days must have been like a man taking a vow of celibacy. Also, I want you to brush up on your dancing for the Havana dream scene." Provocateur gestures with his hands as if imagining the full scope of the sequence.

"Alright. To this, Fidel agrees."

After a few hours of learning the basics and taking breath mints, Finley feels a little more confident. Although he must admit that his co-star Jason is the better dancer.

Everyone applauds at the end of the lesson. "And now, a surprise!" Carla, the dance instructor, announces, "Provocateur is an old partner of mine, and we'd like to show you our award-winning dance...The Tango of Provocation!"

The director dons a fedora and stands atop a folding chair only to descend in a graceful step. He circles Carla in tango-rhythm, and they twist tightly before falling into the classic tango positions.

"Art is provocation!" he exclaims at the finish.

Provocateur goes to great lengths to add authenticity to Fidel Castro's dream sequence. He plans an extravagant shoot in Santo Domingo along an old colonial avenue. Fidel will chase a phantom representing Batista, the corrupt symbol of Capitalism on the island, who will continue to elude him. Fidel will become lost in a maze of slot machines, beautiful dancers, and bright lights that represent various Capitalist temptations he must throw off before becoming the true leader of Cuba.

Finley arrives on set in his khaki uniform. After sitting in hair and makeup, he watches as dozens of extras dressed as bananas seem to wilt in the humid heat. A woman in an astonishing silver glitter monokini smokes a cigarette and laughs at a joke that a mustachioed man is telling her.

"These bananas represent the banana republics of The United States, and Fidel Castro's great antagonist, The United Fruit Company. You must part the sea of dancing bananas and the dancing slot machines, but still the showgirls and the Bolita—the illegal razzle dazzle games—come between you and your true love, Cuba. We have a beautiful dancer, Josefina, to play the part of Cuba, but you have to part the sea of obstacles to reach her." Provocateur instructs points out Finley's path to Josefina.

Finley is to actively avoid dancing with any of the showgirls or "bananas" until he reaches Josefina.

"This dancer, in the 'Tutti Fruitii Hat' represents Miss Chiquita, Carmen Miranda, and the *Good Neighbors* lie." Provocateur points out a dancer who looks very similar to Carmen Miranda. She shakes her hips in a bikini and sarong, her oil-slicked abs glistening in the sun.

Finley kisses her hand in character. "I am charmed by your natural grace and love for Cuba."

She shimmies and grins at him.

Finley runs through it once, but his part is easy. He makes his way through the dancers. He only has to gaze at them with wonder and move past. Miss Carmen gets a long dance solo, and he responds by moving away from her swishes and twirls, his movements a refusal to join her.

A male singer dressed as an American soldier gets a duet with Carmen. The heavy drums of an infectious samba beat pulse in Finley's ears as he continues to move down his own line to Josefina, but several banana-dancers impede his way, and he must hear the soldier-singer's lyrics.

The soldier steps into the spotlight with perfect posture and a fresh face. He waits for the tempo change to begin:

"Good neighbors, spend your heavy labors.
Got to grow bananas with your rhythm and rhyme,
You'll love it, and we'll stay above it.
Got to grow bananas, and you've got to make time.
Oh, me-o, ship them cross the sea-o,
Selling cheap bananas for your nickels and dimes.
Good neighbors building very good republics.
Banana trees will grow like fleas, you'll love it!
Oh, Cuba, what we're doing to ya,
We'll keep singing and taking your fruit from you!"

Carmen and the soldier dance together as the bridge of the song continues. She shimmies around him, clapping. Her verse comes up"

"So happy, Happy to be neighbors.
Thank you for generosity and giving us love.
You love us. Soaring high above us.
Keeping peace like tranquility doves.
So, guide us. Always stay beside us.

We await instruction while we're
Growing big fruit for you!"

Fidel has had enough of this nonsense. Finley motions to stop the song and glares at the talented baritone as if looks could kill. The baritone tips his hat to him and winks. Finley moves him aside with his hand, in what he hopes resembles a clean military thrust, and continues marching to Josefina.

The banana-dancers swirl in Technicolor-yellow all about Fidel, but he pushes one. The bananas fall like Busby Berkeley dominos, then lie still.

Fidel finally reaches Josefina, but she has fallen asleep. He kisses her cheek and cradles her, as if willing her to come alive.

The ruffles on her red gown move gently, and her eyes open.

Fidel rises to see a slot machine behind them.

He picks up a mallet and smashes the glass in the grand finale of the dream sequence.

Weeks before the small-scale Vegas premiere of the indie film *Fidelity*, Provocateur has an idea for publicity. He instructs Finley to meet him in costume at the **Welcome to Las Vegas** sign to hand out fliers. "Che Guevara" insists on also being part of the promotion.

After nearly a year of living in Vegas, Finley hasn't been to the famous landmark. Seeing the familiar neon seems almost spiritual, like a universal touchstone from hundreds of films, existing in some kind of hive mind. Las Vegas itself fills with sand like a beach leading to an endless ocean of casino lights. The sign points the way forward.

Two Elvis impersonators hand out fliers of their own, desperately reaching out to an ocean of potential customers. The impersonators warily eye the actors but reluctantly agree to share the space. It's only one day, after all. Finley makes sure to stand a bit downwind from the smaller Elvis, who wears a faded white jumpsuit—the costume could definitely use a wash or two. The Elvis in the *Comeback Special* black leather look, however, has a dazzling smile and a pleasant reply of "Thank you very much!"

Tourists greet the actors with varying responses. A guy in a Hawaiian shirt, obviously drunk, rages about America and the embargo.

Finley insists that *Fidelity* is a movie that needs to be viewed on its own merits; he refers to it as "my movie" to stay in character.

The guy comes close to shoving Finley, but his friends intervene and carry him back to their Jeep with a California license plate.

Some fans of Provocateur and those with possible Communist sympathies take snapshots with "Fidel." Others give him a shocked look and ignore him. The most memorable encounter happens towards the end of the promotional stunt.

A middle-aged man becomes enraged at the sight of "Fidel" and "Che" in the orange haze of the setting sun. He points a finger straight at Finley. "You son of a bitch! If you really were Fidel Castro, I'd shoot you myself! My father lost every penny after investing in Cuba and died of a broken heart! Why don't you put THAT in your movie?"

"The Revolution is not without cost. I offer my sincere apologies," Finley says in a diplomatic spirit.

The bald man stares for a minute. "Okay, okay, okay. Let me get a picture with you. At least I got to tell Fidel Castro to go to Hell, even if you're not the one in Cuba. Maybe I'll even see the damn movie."

The long afternoon at the **Welcome to Las Vegas** sign seems a non-starter to Finley, but Provocateur views it as a triumph.

He embraces Finley with bear-like intensity. His blue eyes burn with ideas. He paces in semicircles, the flow of inspiration unheeded. "We'll book the steps by The Laga Brutto fountain. You can help with that, of course? First, you write **Cuba** with your finger dipped in water on the fountain. The symbolism! Fidel will reenact the 'History Will Absolve Me' speech. We'll get a dozen peace doves to land on you, and wires to lift you in the sky like a Christ-figure. A single tear can flow down your cheek as you emit profundity."

"For my people," Finley offers. He ignores the Elvis impersonator staring at Provocateur, but it's a cue to leave. "We need to go. We can, uh, plan the dove scene."

"Yes! I need my beret for this! Don't lose the momentum! And find Che Guevara... I thought he was just taking a break, but he split."

Finley, in Fidel Castro regalia, addresses a sparse audience of about 100 in the Laga Brutto courtyard. He writes **CUBA** in water on the fountain's edge, but he's not sure anyone but his director take note. Provocateur instructs him to improvise the speech from memory for spontaneity's sake.

He raises a hand to the crowd. "History will absolve me! The gangsters that overrun Cuba, their putrid slot machines will soon be no more! Parking meters whose coins flow to Batista's cousin! Beady-eyed mobsters sitting in casinos! Cuba needs none of them! I, Fidel, love you and ask only for your fidelity in return. I have battled sharks, gangsters, deceivers, and whores, and now, I give you DOVES OF PEACE!"

Doves land on him as planned. He feels a dove walking in his hair and resists the urge to throw it off his head. The wires lift him along with some of the doves to the second-level balcony where he will wave to "his people."

He can't tell if the crowd is booing or cheering, but he sees Provocateur applauding. Finley takes the stairs down the courtyard, but Provocateur has disappeared.

He'd ridden there with the director, but now he's got to get a taxi in his costume.

He recognizes Sammy, the saxophonist who always seems to be playing by the fountains. He puts a twenty in the hat Sammy leaves on the ground. Sometimes, Finley sings along, and Sammy doesn't seem to mind.

This time, he alters the lyrics a bit to stay in character.

"The smoke of my cigarette hangs in the air,

The fate of my Cuba is beyond all repair,
But, no matter what, I'll rule,
'Cause I'm deep in a dream of me.
Poor Che Guevara didn't survive,
But my brother Raul is okay, so I'll thrive.
I'm the Communist I wanted to be,
'Cause I'm deep in a dream of me."

Provocateur claps nearby, and Finley looks up.

"I didn't know you could sing! I'll try to come up with something for publicity. Hold that thought. Are you ready? I had to round up the doves! We can hand out fliers on the Strip! And we're going to do more speeches with doves... I just had an idea. We could add angel wings and a halo next time." Provocateur seems lost in thought.

"I'll work on that," Finley says, hoping Provocateur will forget about the halo.

The film was not screened for the press. The critics must have brought their knives to cut into prime turkey, but some found the film engaging enough to write a mixed review. The less-than-friendly reception in Cuba actually made Americans more sympathetic to *Fidelity*.

An early screener of the film receives a review from acid-tongued reporter Graham Ginder. In an infamous review of his underground blog, Ginder writes:

"*Somewhere in the story of the Communist revolution in Cuba lies the framework for a great film. Fidelity is not that film. Miscast as Fidel Castro, Finley Luker brings a manic screen presence to the film, suggesting that Castro may have been mentally ill. The smashing of the slot machines, explosions in the jungle, and inane speeches from prison will linger in the viewers' mind like the bite of a jungle mosquito.*"

The premiere of *Fidelity* begins on a mild Vegas evening. The producers prepare for protests. Some have already begun at the local theater. From Cubans to Communists to Conservatives, everyone seems to have opinions about a movie they've never seen. Finley, resembling nothing close to Fidel Castro as a sandy-haired, skinny, blue-eyed Caucasian, retains a degree of anonymity. Only serious fans of his father recognize him. Walking up the row of palm trees, however, he spies a scene far livelier than expected. Somehow, the premiere and his association with Robbie Roberts has caught media attention, and several reporters cue up by the red carpet.

He's waiting for Andrea to arrive for his red carpet-moment.

Stunning in a body-conscious purple bandage dress, flattering makeup on olive skin and black hair as shiny as a Las Vegas night, she holds Finley's hand in quiet support. She whispers to Finley, "As soon as the movie's over, I'm leaving. I'm definitely not going to the after-party with these characters. You know I love you, but Provocateur is too goddamn much." She pulls out a cigarette, lights it, and puffs.

"I thought you quit," he whispers back as cameras click away.

"You drove me back to cigarettes with this movie." She takes another puff.

"You can't smoke in the theater." He looks at the camera and smiles for another picture.

"What are they gonna do? Throw me out?" She poses with a leg out, showing off her gown's daring high slit.

He can only squeeze her a bit harder. "I did this for you. Because I love you."

"Jesus Christ, Finley. Pick a better movie next time." She kisses him for the next photo.

The questions fly like revolutionary bullets. A handful of reporters want to make the most of their time. A small woman in glasses scribbles on a notepad while a blond man with a Caesar haircut poses for pictures before turning to him. "Finley, what do you think of Fidel Castro?" he finally asks.

"He's a figure on the world stage, and his story is history. It's a story that needs to be told."

Another reporter asks a more personal question: "When is the wedding, Finley?"

"October 2005." He squeezes Andrea's hand, and she digs her nails into his palm. He knows she's hating every minute of the premiere and dying for another cigarette even though he wants her to quit.

"Is *Fidelity* a bad movie?" a blunt reporter asks. He's blond with straight teeth and spiked bangs.

"The film will be judged on its merits. I am proud of the film and my acting choices," Finley says, and realizes it's true.

"Is *Fidelity* banned in Cuba?"

"They wouldn't say that, but I don't think it's going to be released there." Finley notices Andrea squirming, so decides to walk off the red carpet. He'll let Jason take it from here. He waves goodbye to the group.

Jason arrives on the red carpet with a model on his arm. Sequins fall from her heavily beaded turquoise gown, but she continues posing. The few photographers snap her picture because she's attractive and largely ignores Jason.

The brunette named Amelie laughs in an open-mouthed fashion and kisses Jason. "Look at me! I'm with Che Guevara!" She lifts a heel in an outrageous pose and kisses Jason on the cheek.

The small reporter in glasses feels enough pity for the movie to pitch a few questions his way. She pushes her glasses further up on her nose and squints. "How would you describe your character in the film?" she reads from a yellow notepad.

"Che Guevara, but all you need to say is Che, and everyone knows him. His real name was Ernesto, but he said, "Umm" so much that they started calling him Umm. Che is Spanish or Portuguese for 'umm,' you see?" Jason loves showing off knowledge of any kind.

The reporter nods to encourage him, but finds him incomprehensible.

Undaunted, Jason continues, "I didn't really study the history because Provocateur had a vision, you know? I've seen posters of Che. I just think of him as Dr. Cool. He was a real doctor, you know? But he was cool. He had a lot of jazz to him. He's got charisma, you got to remember," Jason says, expansively gesturing.

"Jazz? What do you mean by that?" She squints harder.

"Revolution is improv, you know? It's like jazz dance. Except with guns. But we have jazz dance in the film. Bob

Fosse stuff. It's a dream sequence. It's like the *Last Temptation of Christ*, but Fidel is tempted by Capitalism. He and Che dance jazz in a casino with showgirls, but Che finally screams, 'No,' he can't go there. And I knew Che is Dr. Cool. He could probably dance better than anybody. But he's just too moral, you know?" Jason squints in thought.

"Do you think Che had more charisma than Fidel?"

"Oh, absolutely. Fidel needed his Dr. Cool, you know? But they made a great team. I hope that comes out in the film. Me and Finley here, *amigos*. We're like *Butch Cassidy and the Sundance Kid* in Cuba."

Her jaw drops. "Umm... I can't wait to see this movie." Her attention wanders to a spotlight that appears in front of the theater. A drumroll gets louder as the sun sets on the red carpet. A showman in a purple tuxedo approaches a microphone. His real handlebar mustache steals the show. "Ladies and gentlemen! Our film's director, Provocateur, wants to personally welcome you to the film! To show how revolutionary the film is, he will be shot out of a cannon before your very eyes! Look to your left, and he will land on the net to your far right!"

Provocateur waves to the crowd and gets into the cannon. He's dressed like a vaudeville acrobat.

Finley bites his lip, hoping the stunt won't result in grievous injury.

Provocateur sails through the air, arms rigid at his sides in a breathtaking display.

The stunt goes perfectly, and he waves to a shocked crowd. Wiping perspiration off with a monogrammed handkerchief, Provocateur passes by Finley and Jason. He stops to rally his actors. He claps a hand over each actor's shoulder in jubilation. "Now you may see the complete film we have made! I have never been prouder of a film. You are my innovators! Always remember, creativity dances with desperation!"

Palm trees frame the entrance to the theater. They head inside to see their movie for the first time. Finley takes an assigned seat right in front of the massive screen. He's about to experience his performance as any other moviegoer—with popcorn, too. He's seen himself as one of the kids on *The*

Marshmallow Show years ago, but *Fidelity* is his project about to emerge from its chrysalis, either to take flight or fall on its face.

His Fidel resembles something mad, but Finley can't take his eyes off the screen. Fidel's camaraderie with Che has potential for accidental comedy, and already he can hear chuckles from the audience, especially when Fidel starts referring to himself in third person or ranting about the dangers of slot machines. Finley feels that the movie may not be perfect, but it has its own way of commanding attention.

THE ASSASSINATION OF A BULLFIGHTER

Finley sits in Glenda Samuelson's Los Angeles office, eyeing its multitude of potted cacti. He notices a decorative fence, tumbleweed, and a sign that says, **The Headshot Corral**. He sees the familiar headshot of Kevin Luker with a fedora in one hand and an open-mouth smile. Marshmallow has her own headshot; he sees where his father scribbled in broad cursive, *Some bunny loves you, Marshmallow.*

He scans down the angled rows of black-and-white headshots. There's Ann Kiefer, a brunette who played jilted wives and bitter mothers. You wouldn't know her career hadn't quite taken off from the ebullient yellow swimsuit in her famous sailboat cheesecake photo. She's wearing red shoes and keeping her straw hat from blowing off in the wind.

His eyes move past Ann's headshot to the next row. Many of the faces seem familiar, but most of the headshots are anonymous strangers captured in one moment of their lives on the agent's wall. He looks at one framed photograph that seems more than recognizable. He's shocked to see a younger Scott Todd in a serious-looking headshot from the '80s. Finley thought of Scott as Mr. Sparkle's spouse and pianist, not an aspiring young actor. The photo looks like a still frame from a *Sherlock Holmes* TV show, complete with a pipe and armchair.

He must be right about the *Sherlock Holmes* part; Scott signed it, *Elementary, my dear Glenda, xoxo - Scott Todd.* Finley knows little of handwriting analysis, but he'd love to know what the tight, small letters mean.

"Finley Luker, let's have a look at you!" Glenda gives him one of her famous hugs. "How are you?"

He hugs her back a little, and they walk into her office. Its red-and-blue color scheme seems downright tasteful after the loud waiting room. He sits on an overstuffed yellow chair and spills his guts as if she's his new therapist. "I'm at loose ends. Dad's death was sudden, and I feel like I've lost Marshmallow, too. Sometimes I hated her, but she was kind of like a sister. And now *Fidelity* is over..." Finley lets the sentence trail off, as if stopping himself from going too far.

"Well, Provocateur is filming an anti-bullfighting film in Spain, and I assumed you wouldn't want to film too far from your fiancée. Not with the wedding so close and all." Glenda pauses to watch his reaction.

Finley nods to show he's listening.

She plunges ahead, "He's assured me that he's willing to work with you again in the future. He's very impressed with your 'visceral questing,' as he put it." Glenda opens a giant day planner.

Finley waits for the next statement.

"I can't call *Fidelity* a roaring success, but you've... uh...made an impression. I've got a script for a film set in the Vietnam War era about a young man dodging the draft in Canada. It's sort of a marijuana film. It's not really my cup of tea, but you could take a look at it. It's the new Jeff Savoie film. It's got buzz all over it." On her office chair, she rolls over to a filing cabinet and swivels to retrieve her copy. She hands him the script.

He notices the highlighted lines stop halfway through the story.

"Of course, you wouldn't be the lead this time, but there is quite a death scene," she adds. "Death scenes can really make a stir in Hollywood. I mean, think of Gary Cooper in the silent movie version of *Beau Geste*. His death scene was so moving that, ten years later, he starred in the remake as the lead."

"Huh," Finley says without looking up. "I'm interested. Is it a comedy?" He notices his character has a monologue about houseplants on page 63.

"I'm really not sure. Maybe it's like M*A*S*H or something, and I'm just not getting the jokes."

He nods, reading over lines that sound like Shakespeare compared to *Fidelity*. He'd still like to give that scriptwriter a piece of his mind.

"Now, let's talk about an updated headshot. But, maybe while you're in L.A., you can see the hairstylist first. Marc Rivera gives my clients a discount, and he can make you the next Brad Pitt. I'd love to schedule that for tomorrow. We'll provide you with suitable clothes."

Finley looks down at his Hawaiian shirt and jeans, coloring a bit at the perceived jibe, but Glenda has a point.

"Do you still run every day?" Glenda asks, chewing on a ballpoint pen.

"About four days a week."

"Lift weights?" She takes the pen out of her mouth as if remembering to curb bad habits.

"Is there a certain fitness regimen for this film?" Finley leans forward in the office chair.

"The character is a soldier, Finley. So, maybe a military-type regimen until filming begins next month."

"Don't I have to audition?" His eyebrow lift.

"Oh, the casting director watched *Fidelity* and said that was all she needed."

"You don't say."

The sun beats down, and Finley can feel sweat begin to drip from his forehead and cover his forearms. Running in Death Valley isn't uncommon, he reassures himself, and he's not a novice runner. It's a dry heat. He tries to convince his body that it's comfortable.

The air becomes almost visible in extreme heat. He can see it vibrating in pace with him. The desert horizon stretches toward infinity as his feet move on autopilot. He observes his pace and breath as if he is an astral projection of himself. Despite the pain and effort, he banks on a euphoria that he only gets from running.

It's been 40 minutes in a planned ten-mile run. He sees something in white to the left of his path. It takes shape as he runs towards it. Something incredible looms beside a cactus. Elvis has fallen from the sky in the desert, white jumpsuit gleaming. He stares at Finley with intensity.

"'*Burning Love*,'" Elvis screams. He holds his arms above his head and makes peace signs. Elvis isn't standing on the ground. He stands mid-air, almost a foot above the sand.

Finley swerves then makes a U-turn. He's having a heat hallucination already. He looks behind him after a moment and sees no trace of Elvis. He falls to one knee near a solitary cactus and decides to lie in the sand. After all, no one is around to see him except a few lizards.

Somehow, he makes it back to his car. After sitting in the air-conditioning, waiting for his ears to stop pulsing, he calls Glenda.

She doesn't pick up, so he leaves a voicemail.

"If the offer is still available, I want to do the bullfighting movie with Provocateur..."

"Finley, as the assassin Sebastian Gering, murders the bullfighter, José Hernandez, in a karmic paroxysmal impulse. The repeated murder of bulls has led to José's death. He dies as a result of sin against animals, against nature itself. We're planning a vivid half-hour montage of this character's demise by the most violent means possible. You will play the assassin's role," Provocateur's voice bellows over the phone, his excitement about a new project audible even on a long-distance call.

"Why does my character want to assassinate the bullfighter?" Finley asks with genuine curiosity.

"It is set in the 1970s in fascist Spain. The bullfighter is sponsoring Communists in Cuba financially, and the assassin has been sent by Franco himself. The dictator knows he cannot afford to have the citizenry know the most famous man in Spain is a Communist. You must kill the bullfighter or be killed by dictator Franco!"

"Oh, Communism again. I've had some experience on my last movie." Finley laughs. "What's the wardrobe like?"

Provocateur ignores the laugh and continues in a serious tone. "This will be nothing like *Fidelity*. I'm trying a different approach. We made that movie too quickly. We're going to slow things down. We will employ meditation and team-building. I have excursions planned to develop what will appear on screen. Even your costume will be dramatic. You will have slicked-back hair and dark glasses. We will see your real nose this time. You will wear trench coats and porkpie hats."

Finley imagines Provocateur miming the shape of a porkpie hat around his head. "Won't the bullfighter be suspicious?"

"His arrogance precludes any fear from assassins. He believes he is a god, really. I was thinking of our friend Jason for the part."

"Wow. I'm sure he'll love it." Finley mulls this over. "What about the assassination scene? It lasts for quite a while in the script."

"It is the glorious set-piece for the film. The very heart of it! You will loom behind José with a corkscrew that you will force into his skull! But his death will be long and theatrical." Provocateur pauses.

Finley hears female voices shouting in Spanish and guitar music in the background.

The director continues, "We have much to do. When can you get to Barcelona? I'm researching principal photography and costumes."

Finley doubts Provocateur's claim about being engaged in "research" from the party sounds but doesn't let the director know. "I'm going to take Andrea out to a tapas restaurant and really sell the idea of a Spanish honeymoon. If it works, I can be there by October 12th."

"Good luck, Finley. *Au revoir*."

Finley tries to keep track of his schedule for the new film and his wedding as the days approach.

Provocateur flies back to Sin City for Finley's wedding and to work out the casting for *The Assassination of a Bullfighter*. Although Provocateur plans to do most filming in Barcelona, another producer suggests changing the setting of the climactic bullfight to Mexico City. Regardless, Provocateur plans to make use of the *Fidelity* crew in Las Vegas. Finley will take on the lead role as the murderer. Provocateur hopes to add edge to the film by shooting the assassination from the killer's point of view.

Finley's character, Sebastian, will dine at the bullfighter's *hacienda* and befriend him, all the while planning to murder him. The bullfighter, José, will talk about raising chickens and rustic life, never knowing his assassin is looming behind him.

Finley lies on Mr. Sparkle's velvet settee in a sunroom, reading the first known copy of the script. Provocateur tried his hand at writing it, and a myriad of notations line the margins of the pithy tome. Finley comes to his character's first interaction with the doomed bullfighter on page 43.

Sebastian: Tell me about the old days, José. When you first acquired fame and tasted of the victories over Spain's wildest bulls.

José: It is like these chickens I keep. They are weak and meant to be feasted upon. It is no different with the bull. Except the bull has horns and presents a danger to the bullfighter. Perhaps not like chickens at all, eh? I have looked into the eyes of beasts that meant to gore me with their horns. I have flashed my red cape to tempt their fury!

Sebastian: But there are times when a bullfighter loses the fight. When the bull injures him. Every bullfighter must remain on guard.

José: Yes, but I never lose! This you will see at my next bull fight. I am undefeated by any bull in the world. Tonight, I extend my conquests to the rustic life and to entertaining guests at my *hacienda*!

Sebastian: Then a toast to your long life.

José: Yes, a toast with the reddest wine in Barcelona!

"Are you reading another script?" Andrea's voice startles Finley. "*The Assassination of a Bullfighter* by Provocateur?" she reads the cover page in disbelief.

"I wanted to talk about this," Finley starts. "I was planning to tell you today."

"Where is it filming? And when? Are you insane?" She rages at him with her eyes.

"Have you ever been to Barcelona? We could have our honeymoon first... I was going to take you out for tapas." He puts the script aside.

"Yeah, you're taking me out for tapas. And while you're running around Europe, making god-awful movies with a crazy Commie, I'll be calling up George in Milan. He asked me to model, and that's where I'll go while you're acting! Maybe it's time I start focusing on MY career instead of Mr. Sparkle's and yours!" She paces and throws her hands up for emphasis.

"You should model. You're beautiful. You can do anything you want with your career." He kisses her on the forehead.

She calms down a bit at that. "There's so many bags to pack. I've got to go shopping!" Andrea strides out of the sunroom towards her beloved Louis Vuitton trunks. "Don't wait up for me tonight."

Finley looks forward to breaking away from wedding preparations to go to the table read for *Assassination of a Bullfighter*. The film, no longer secret to his fiancée, moves forward in circuitous increments as an international shoot must be planned.

Jason sits at the long table with a pencil and his script, jotting character notes in the margins. He sports a new goatee and mustache that look a bit Spanish. "Have you ever seen a bullfight, Finley? Do you think we should attend one in Spain for research?"

"That could be helpful." Finley opens his script and reads the opening scene.

Provocateur strides into the conference room and places monogrammed water bottles in front of each actor: **FL** for Finley and **JK** for Jason. "I've commissioned a VW microbus and a meditation leader, Soleil, for our trip to the mesa today. We will have more water on the bus. We're going to center and focus on solitude within the actor's circle to extrude the best selves within our spheres." Provocateur scribbles illegible notes into a turquoise notebook and marks something on a checklist.

"I thought this was a table read," Finley says in dismay.

"Do you really think I'm the kind of director to stay in a conference room? I've seen rocks more inspiring than this beige nightmare of a room. We'll get to the script, but you've got to do the inner work first!" He points to his own solar plexus and claps Finley on the back in his enthusiasm.

Jason grins at Finley. "This is fantastic. I love getting out into nature. Let's get in the microbus!"

They see a blonde dressed in a white scarf, tie-dyed leggings, and a sports bra texting on her cell phone and looking bored. She keeps the A/C running in the rusted microbus. Soleil fastens her seat belt and opens the sliding door when she sees the actors approach. Her voluminous social smile reveals perfect white teeth. "Good mesa morning! I'm ecstatic to be your meditation guide today," she says as they get into the car. "Aren't you going to fasten your seat belt?" she chides Finley. "Mindfulness starts in small ways. Enjoy the inspiring vistas and this CD of Tibetan yak bells and my other CD of humpback whale songs as we approach our destination."

"How long will our, umm, journey be?" Finley wonders how long he'll be stuck in this vehicle.

"We should arrive at the mesa in about an hour." Her CD begins with a female voice explaining how the yaks are ceremoniously decorated, and even Finley must admit that the sound of bells creates an eerie effect. It would be soothing if the yak noises didn't disrupt the bells so much.

He watches the scenery unfold like an orange and tan diorama. He sinks into a half-reverie; although his style of meditation may not be what his director has in mind. The transition from the bell sounds to the whale CD jars him, and he looks over at Jason who slurps a Coca-Cola. He notices the microbus pulling over to an enormous mesa. "How are we getting up?" Finley looks high up the layered rock.

"There're hooks for the climbing equipment on the north face," Soleil says.

"Climbing equipment? I've only climbed a fake rock wall at the mall, and that was years ago." Finley also hates heights, but he doesn't say it.

"Acting is a leap of faith. Meditation is work. So, we climb the mesa." Soleil nods.

"Come on, Finley. Let's harness up. Last one up is a rotten egg." Jason seems to grin at the chance to outshine his costar to impress Soleil and Provocateur. "Once I'm up there, I'm going to meditate hard."

"No, we're all going to relax and enjoy the splendor of the desert hues. Just inhale purity and exhale contamination. Don't worry, I'm a licensed climber and a professional photographer." Soleil squints, looking for the best spot on the mesa for lighting the promotional photos.

After some instruction from Soleil, Finley adjusts to the harness and recalls his remedial knowledge of climbing. He can see the flat-top hill towering at around 1,000 feet, surrounded by the Sierra Nevada Mountains. Jason climbs above him, and the sand below them begins to recede. He moves up the pink-and-beige-layered mesa and forgets about the height as he climbs. The air waves and hums with the intense desert heat. Jason slips down a bit, and a startled Finley reaches up to steady him. Finley has good reflexes when he forgets to be nervous.

Soleil spreads out yoga mats on top of the mesa and begins with a basic yoga pose. The less flexible men attempt to mimic her, but Finley decides to lie on the mat and stare at the cirrus cloud display. He floats as if the mesa were made of air, and he feels a oneness with the mountains. He exists with them. He visualizes his happy place: the bedroom he shares with Andrea. He begins visualizing more distracting images that have everything to do with Andrea and nothing to do with meditation.

He refocuses on the desert air around him. His arms, slick with sweat, belie the repeated notion of "dry heat." He realizes he's been tuning out Soleil and tries to reengage with her guided meditation.

"The mesa becomes a plateau. The notion of plateau steadies our energy. We remain still and engaged in the earth if we ground ourselves like the mesa. The surface area touches the desert but longs for the water. We let the water of meditation rain on our parched consciousness." Soleil speaks in soothing tones as if she has said these words many times.

Soleil succeeds in reminding Finley that he does thirst, and he reaches in his pack for the monogrammed water bottle. He can taste a hint of cucumber. He glances over at Provocateur and Jason. Provocateur has taken on the happy baby yoga pose and his eyes close in an expression of bliss. Jason, over to Finley's left, furrows his brow and texts on his flip phone. He notices Finley, raises an eyebrow, and returns to texting.

The minutes tick by, and Finley feels the effects of the heat more than the calm of meditation. After moments of interminable stillness, Provocateur shifts and sits, looking at the mountains and the sand and the turquoise vista. At last, he speaks, "You might wonder what the purpose of our journey has been. You expected to read through a script, and I led you to unexpected heights. But this was my intention. We are team-building and building trust. We must be a team and go to Spain with a singular vision. I must lead this team. A director is like a god on Mount Olympus, guiding the actors to create the magic of film. And I believe we have found the seeds of magic on this mesa." Provocateur speaks with the gravitas of a man who believes his own words. "And I want to thank our meditation leader, Soleil Rivers, for making this day possible."

Soleil stands and rolls up her yoga mat. "We will descend the mesa with great care and respect for the peace she has bestowed on us."

Finley feels that the two expect a response, and he stands to roll his yoga mat, mirroring Soleil. "Thank you, Soleil, and thank you, Provocateur. Yesterday, I could say I had never climbed a mesa, but now I have. I've never met anyone as unforgettable as my director. I can't wait to get to Barcelona." He shakes Soleil's hand in awkward formality.

She beams at him.

Jason rolls up his mat as well, squinting at his phone. "My battery's almost dead. I'm starving. Can we end our journey at a restaurant?"

Provocateur stares at Jason for a moment. "There's a great Tex-Mex place on the way home. Or we could find a Denny's."

The descent from the mesa, while still terrifying, finds Finley more relaxed. Although supported by the harness, he finds a spiritual dimension while suspended in thin air, taking an aerial view of the desert. The abyss below him stretches to infinite, sand-colored horizons.

He unbuckles and hears a heated conversation between Soleil and Provocateur. Jason sits with the door of the microbus open, hydrating himself and looking around.

"Jason is integral to my vision of this film," Provocateur says with solemn authority.

"He has a negative aura. He didn't meditate, and he didn't attempt to participate!" Soleil paces.

"This film exudes violence and hatred. There must be energies other than peaceful ones to provide the necessary conflict to the story. His unique viewpoint will be part of my panorama." Provocateur frames the desert with his hands and rotates the view to illustrate his point. "You succeeded in the exercise today, no matter what energy Jason brought to it. We have gone further into our imaginative questing." The director grips her shoulders.

"Yes! I can see you are right." She embraces Provocateur, and Finley wonders if their relationship has gone beyond professional. The embrace deepens into a kiss. He feels a bit voyeuristic and walks over to the microbus, satisfied that the conflict has been resolved, happy it won't affect the movie. He retrieves his copy of the ever-evolving script and rereads the dialogue on page eleven for the fiftieth time. He tries to make the assassin's flowery language feel organic. He must become murderous and unhinged in his performance.

Soon, Jason walks over, slurping from his water bottle. "Have you memorized your lines yet?"

"I'm not off book, if that's what you mean."

Jason doesn't answer and looks over at Soleil and Provocateur in their heated embrace. He says, "I should have known he didn't just hire her for her skills."

"I think meditation might be good for Provocateur. Maybe it will inspire him."

"Maybe he'll write a better script someday."

"What's your problem?"

"I'm hungry, and it's a burning desert out here, or haven't you noticed? And they're oblivious to my suffering."

"Great suffering brings greater art."

"Who are you quoting? Ibsen?"

"I just made it up. Sounded good, right? We've got to calm down. You made it down from the mesa, right? We're so close to being done and back in Vegas."

"Finley, you're almost as crazy as they are, but you have a point."

Provocateur and Soleil walk towards the microbus, their steps in synch. With clasped hands, Provocateur looks over at Soleil as if to make an announcement. She seems to nod, as if prodding him.

"We will take our leave from this mesa, but first, Soleil would like to burn sage to purify the aura here and reassure the mesa of our positive intention. I want to congratulate both of you on completing the exercise. I believe if we become cohesive and grounded, we can far surpass our previous work of *Fidelity*." Provocateur takes a deep breath and one last look at the vast expanse around them.

Finley looks over to Jason as if expecting an interruption, but Jason looks ahead as if he'd been meditating all along. He watches as Soleil burns the sage, shaking the ashes towards each member but pausing over Jason the longest.

"We'll have to repeat this exercise before our Spanish journey begins." Provocateur looks at the group to gauge their response.

Jason nods. "I've never felt closer to any team than I do right now. It's almost a spiritual intensity."

Soleil gives a wide smile and gives Jason a hug. "You don't know how happy you've made me!"

The microbus makes its way out of the desert, and Soleil turns the dial to a classic rock station instead of the yak CD. Jason sits with an enigmatic expression, and Finley can't tell if he had really been honest with Soleil. He can smell the cannabis wafting from Provocateur's seat and asks if he can take a puff. Finley likes the herbal taste of pot but never the vague sort of high that results from smoking too much. He'd never say that to Provocateur's face. This pot tastes like oregano and sweet basil.

Soleil turns into a Tex-Mex place called The Three Little Pigs, and Finley waits for everyone to exit before stepping out on wobbly legs. The sunset beams its colors across the sky, and he feels exhilarated.

Jason gets a booth before anyone can stop him and orders an Anaheim chili bowl with Fritos and gooey cheese.

"I will have no queso for I have climbed the mesa," Provocateur recites a line he's made up as if quoting *King Lear*.

"What are you going to eat?" Jason looks up from the menu.

"I think the street tacos will do. What about you, Finley? Or you, Soleil?"

"I think I'll have dessert for dinner. It's a calorie-saving device, you know." Soleil looks at a picture of the tres leches cake with longing.

Provocateur continues, "I'd really like to know how my actors feel in this moment. And we need to always be in the present. Jason, I know you don't always feel heard, and I'd like to hear any thoughts you may have on the progress of the film before we depart for Spain."

"Part of me knows the mesa was beautiful, and meditation is good for me, and maybe I even felt something. But then there's part of my brain that wants to shut down on it because it's not my style. Acting is from the gut. You stand there, and you've got to feel something." Jason exhales a bit.

"What about you, Finley?"

"The experience of the mesa took me out of my comfort zone. I never really climbed before, but there's something pure about looking at the world from a different perspective. And we've got another mountain to climb when it comes to making this film. I can't put it into words, but I feel purpose. Mostly, I feel peace."

"That's the most beautiful thing I've ever heard, mister. Wow." The waitress looks at Finley in awe. "Did you order the chili and Fritos?"

"That would be me." Jason raises his hand.

"Sure. I'll be right back." She keeps smiling at Finley all the way back to the kitchen. She turns around after nearly colliding with a waiter. An enormous tray of enchiladas nearly drops to the floor.

Provocateur takes a drink of water and clears his throat. He squeezes Soleil's hand for support and takes a deep breath. "Finley, we're making progress. Our experience at the mesa has been esemplastic. We proceed with one mind, with the intention of creating a film. This genesis will create the momentum to carry us to Barcelona. We must follow the call. There is a lodge nearby, The Coyote's Paw. The simplicity of nature will inspire us. I suggest we stay there for a few days. Soleil has volunteered to lead us in yoga and meditation."

Finley pauses. He knows he will have to make a phone call to Andrea, but Jason already has an answer:

"Yes. Let's do it!"

"*Namaste*," Soleil adds. "I hear there's a nature trail and zip line. Bike rentals if anyone is interested."

Jason turns his attention to the chili the waitress has just delivered. He starts drinking out of his glass in desperation and turns red as radishes.

"Spicy hot? They didn't begin to warn me about this. It's lethal!"

"Maybe just eat the Fritos then, Finley suggests. "You did order the ghost pepper chili. That's the hottest pepper, I think."

"I need to get to The Coyote's Paw ASAP. And I need a glass of milk."

"Here. Take a bit of this cake. I think it will soothe the inflammation." Soleil holds out a forkful of the creamy dessert.

Jason chews it slow, and his face looks less beet-colored after a few seconds.

"You really are a healer," Jason rasps after a minute.

After Provocateur takes care of the check, the group heads back to the microbus. Finley notices Jason staring at him, but whenever he turns to make eye contact, Jason turns away. Soleil and Provocateur seem to be lost, and everyone needs some sleep after a strenuous day.

"The Coyote's Paw used to be here. I guess they changed ownership. Let's just stay here tonight then."

No one disagrees, and she continues into the lodge. Soleil squints at the buildings as she parks the microbus. The sign out front reads, **The Bare Bones Hostel**, and Finley shudders at the name.

Decorative skulls dot the walls and displays of cacti rim the main office. A giant stuffed bear greets them at the front door. Its lifeless, glassy eyes seem to warn Finley to run.

"Do you have any vacancies?" Provocateur asks the man at the front desk.

"Oh, yes. Indeed. We have vacancies. It's wonderful to welcome guests...especially the lovely woman," the tall, thin man with leathery skin answers. He wears his gray hair in a ponytail despite his receding hairline.

"We'll need three rooms, please. The lady and I will share a room and these gentlemen will need separate accommodations. You can put them on my bill."

The clerk opens a guestbook. "Please sign in. The rooms are ready. We're not very busy... this time of year, you know. Vacancies. Too many vacancies." The man, whose name tag reads **Sergio**, blinks a few times. He seems to be staring at Soleil.

"You don't have to do that. I can pay for my room," Finley protests.

"Finley, I am your director, and I consider this weekend an invaluable synergistic opportunity for wellness. Please allow me to take care of my actors." Provocateur signs his name with an enormous **P** and the last name **Johnson**.

"Are you making a movie?" the clerk asks. "I love movies. I'm a big documentary fan myself. Anything involving nature or wellness." He smiles at Soleil.

"We are in preparation for a movie we will film in Spain. We need to center our creative energies before the process begins," Provocateur says with simmering enthusiasm.

"We've got a yoga room. And a sauna. If you meditate in the sauna, it's kind of spiritual, like a sweat lodge, you know? Purifying. Nobody's used it since...since...for a while. You'll need a map to get around the place." Sergio hands them a colorful brochure.

Soleil perks up as Sergio mentions holistic amenities. "Thank you, Sergio. I'm sure we'll be very comfortable here."

"Oh, you're welcome. Very welcome, indeed." Sergio's lips stretch into a strange smile.

Finley feels alarm at the strange lobby and its strange occupant, but no one else seems concerned. He decides that he will never step foot into the sauna, no matter what Provocateur says.

"Let's head back to the bus. You can access anything you want to take to your room." Provocateur commands the group while looking at the map. He and Finley walk a bit faster than Jason and Soleil. "There's a nature trail. I suggest you and Jason meet up in the lobby for a morning hike. There's nothing more rejuvenating than a walk in nature. And it's a good opportunity for you and Jason to really work through your issues. Soleil and I will do our morning yoga, as usual, and we can meet up in the lobby and go from there."

"Hiking's fine with me," Jason says. "As long as Finley can keep up."

Finley doesn't respond. He grabs his monogrammed water bottle before heading to his room. "Goodnight, you guys."

He squints to find the right room number before opening the door into the dimly lit entryway. Outside his room, dozens of moths fly around a buzzing lantern, but he's surprised to see a rather handsome leather chair and an artfully rendered painting of a coyote staring over a traditional wooden bed. A Southwestern quilt hangs over the bed that seems clean enough, and a slight hint of pine wafts through the air. The coyote's eyes in the painting across from the bed follow him, but Finley soon drifts off to sleep after a day full of exertion.

In the morning, Finley wakes up at around 4:30AM. He stares for a while at the black alarm clock on the nightstand. Unable to sleep, he gets dressed for the morning hike. He wonders if he's too early for breakfast; he knows Provocateur often wakes by sunrise. Finley decides to knock on Provocateur's suite, aware not to make too much noise, although he doesn't think any other guests are at the hotel.

Provocateur opens to door. He holds an old-fashioned wooden palette and wears his beret. He goes back to an astonishing six-foot canvas depicting a bullfighter waving a red flag at a bull with its powerful front legs up in the air.

"Good morning. I woke up early. I wanted to check in. I didn't know you painted," Finley says.

"Art takes many forms. Painting was the first form that entranced my senses. I return to it for therapy and to infuse my films with its dynamic visual impetus. Every shot of this film will be a work of art. Every frame will be the visual equivalent of an oil painting. Bullfighting, though morally reprehensible, fuses art and death. The assassination of the bullfighter symbolizes the ironic fate of humanity; we flicker like decorative candles, but our flames can be snuffed out in a moment. Dying is art in synthesis."

"What is my assassin's role then? My character is not in the painting." Finley steps back to look at the whole canvas.

"The assassin is death personified. Your character is in the painting. He is the fear in the bull's eyes. He is the red of the flag which symbolizes blood yet to be spilled. He is the fear in the bullfighter's eyes even as he moves to victory; he knows that one false move could result in his death. Yes, let me make the eyes more terrified here, right here in the bull's pupil." Provocateur takes a palette knife and slashes and scrapes white paint off the canvas. He then mixes a bit of brown and black paint, adds an eyelash to the bull's expressive face.

"Do you mind if I watch you paint for a while? I'm a little early for hiking." Finley doesn't know if Jason has woken up or if he's even in the lobby.

"Of course. The painting will inform your performance in Spain. That was our whole purpose behind climbing the mesa."

Finley sits on a leather chair and watches Provocateur for a while. The director has some skill with the brush and captures expressions and movement well. After several minutes spent observing small changes in the bull's eyes, Finley looks at his watch and realizes it's time to hike. "I'll see you in a little while."

Provocateur does not look away from the bull's face. "*Au revoir.*"

The lobby door is open, and Finley finds Jason sitting on an overstuffed chair. The breakfast seems very continental, meaning it consists only of instant coffee and stale doughnuts. Finley drinks the scalding-hot liquid without cream or sugar, from a Styrofoam cup.

Jason has penciled circular lines on his lodge map. "I've mapped out the best route. There's a spot called Coyote Ridge with a lookout tower. We can hike to that and circle back."

"That sounds fine. As long as we stay away from that sauna."

"Yeah." Since Sergio sits at the desk across the hall Jason drops his voice. "What do you think is up with that? He got kind of weird when he mentioned it."

"Maybe... Maybe somebody died in the sauna. Maybe he turned up the heat on purpose. You know, kind of like Norman Bates except with the sauna instead of a shower."

"Are you serious? This guy's no Norman Bates. He's just a sleazeball," Jason laughs. "And we didn't steal any money."

"Well, you can never be too careful. Maybe we'll be safer out on the trail with the coyotes." Finley notes the inn's arched doorway and some Spanish gothic-style benches as they walk out of the lobby. They follow a gravel path lined with cacti towards a faded trail marker.

Scraggly trees and cacti dot the trail as the sun beats down on the two hikers. Lizards scurry out, and the wind makes noises as it rolls over the dust around them. After a couple of miles, Finley starts to worry that Jason may have gotten them lost, but he notices his hiking companion checking the map from time to time. He spies a rickety lookout tower and balks at climbing it.

"We've come all the way out here. Let's give it a go," Jason says before Finley can raise an objection.

"I guess," Finley says.

They climb the spiral stairs to the top. An ancient telescope sits there near a roughhewn bench. The wind howls at an amplified volume, but Finley can see the mesa they'd climbed the day before and the roads carved out of the rock below them. Jason looks through the telescope as Finley observes the landscape with the naked eye.

As Finley looks towards a hill adjacent the tower, he notices a ragged coyote standing with its eyes turned towards him. The coyote steps forward in curiosity. Finley sees the hispid-textured fur, the beige fringes spotted with gray. The hazel eyes of the creature stare into his eyes. Finley wonders if the coyote might be his spirit animal; he's been alone in the wilderness like the coyote, but somehow, he's survived. The animal turns away and runs off into the distance.

The tower sways a bit, and even Jason has to admit that it might be safer on the ground.

"Time to go." Finley starts walking down the spiral staircase. He wonders why he didn't point out the coyote to Jason, but then reflects that the coyote is his spirit animal. Jason can get his own spirit animal.

As they walk into the hotel, Finley notices that Sergio has a sullen look, and then, he notices the innkeeper also has a black eye. He sees Soleil and Provocateur sitting in the lobby. Provocateur has an arm around Soleil, and no one seems to be talking. The director's stark-black hair hangs over his face like a fringe to hide his eyes.

"We just got back from the hike. Are we checking out already?" Finley asks his director.

"Yes. We want to leave as soon as possible." Provocateur looks up and glares at Sergio. "We'll be in the microbus."

"What do you think happened?" Finley asks Jason in the corridor as they walk to their respective rooms.

"One of them decked that creep. He was probably creeping on Soleil or maybe even Provocateur, or both, in the yoga room. He wasn't murdering anyone in the sauna. But I think he's been trying to get a little too close to his female guests. I hope he gave us a discount at least." Jason looks thoughtful.

"I don't want to know. It would be a nice place under different ownership though. The trail's alright." After a few minutes, Finley walks through the lobby. He doesn't want to look at Sergio, but the innkeeper stares at him.

"I hope you enjoyed your stay," Sergio says in a strained voice.

"The nature trail was...illuminating. Thank you." Finley walks fast to get back to the microbus. He sees Jason already sitting in the back, listening to something with heavy bass riffs on his headphones.

"To close our meditative weekend, I have another CD. This is a relaxing medley of ocean sounds and seagulls." Soleil adjusts her mirror and fastens her seatbelt. "We'll head back to the conference room in Vegas, of course, so you can get back to your vehicles."

Provocateur gives Soleil a soothing pat on the arm. "I want to thank these fine actors for stepping into the abyss, the wilderness of the mind, and retrieving clarity."

Finley clears his throat; he's ready to open up about his breakthrough. "I think I found my spirit animal while hiking. I saw a coyote on a hill across from the lookout tower. His eyes looked into mine for a moment, and I felt a...connection."

Jason turns away, and Finley can't be sure if he's stifling laughter. "Are you sure your spirit animal is a coyote? I would have thought maybe a llama or a penguin, maybe."

"I'm not sure what it means. Maybe that I've made it through my own personal wilderness. It just has to be more than a coincidence. I had left my room that morning, and the coyote's eyes in the portrait seemed to follow me. Maybe it's a sign, a good one," Finley defends, refusing to let Jason bring him down.

Soleil interjects, "That's really great, Finley. That's a wonderful sentiment to end our journey to the mesa and beyond."

Jason clears his throat. "I didn't feel positive about climbing a mesa when our...journey began. It was because...when I was a teenager, I experienced a UFO near a mesa. I still don't know how to handle it. But I'm glad that I can see mesas in a better way. From now on."

Finley is shocked hearing this and can't think of anything to say. He'd never thought of Jason as being troubled by anything.

Soleil looks at Jason through the rearview mirror. "You know, that was very vulnerable to admit. I'm really impressed right now. Being vulnerable is a first step to receiving positive energy. I think we're ready to go to Spain and make a wonderful film with this amazing director. And I can give you some contact information for a support group of other UFO-experiencers just like you. There's a group that meets in Vegas on Wednesday nights."

"I think that could help me. Thanks." Jason exhales as if his tension melts away.

Finley drifts to sleep as the humpback whales sing on the CD in the background. He wakes up after the microbus pulls into the office parking lot. Provocateur has chosen an upstairs office right next to a Whole Foods-centered mini-mall.

A blonde producer Finley knows only as Amy rushes to Provocateur and Soleil. "You have a visitor. He insisted on waiting for you in the conference room."

"Who is it? Perhaps a wealthy Spanish financier with an offer to distribute the film?" Provocateur strokes his black beard, lost in thought.

"He said his name is Jeff Savoie. I think he's a producer?" Amy squints as she tries to remember any movies with his name attached.

"Should we wait until you've seen him to go in the room?" Finley wonders.

"No. I'm sure you're tired from our journey. I'll get you a new copy of the script if you'll just wait a moment."

Finley walks past Amy and Soleil as the two women speak in hushed voices. Provocateur strides into the conference room, followed by Jason.

A silver-haired man with black-framed glasses sits at the conference table, reading the script. His crisp blue suit and red tie command attention, as does his exemplary posture. The man looks up then stands to greet Provocateur. "Forgive the intrusion, gentlemen. You see, I offered a young, unknown actor a chance to appear in a film of mine. He turned me down cold. Said he wanted to work with a director named Provocateur on a film about a bullfighter being murdered. I think the actor's name was Finley Luker. I wanted to see what all the fuss was about. Allow me to introduce myself. I'm Jeff Savoie." Savoie extends a hand to Provocateur and then to Finley.

"And...how may we help you? I see you're reading the script." Provocateur looks at his visitor with piqued curiosity.

"I can honestly say that I've never read anything like it before." Savoie laughs, then stops himself when he sees the director's serious look. "I won't trouble you much longer, but let me give you my card. Your last film got some attention. We should do lunch someday if you're ever in Los Angeles."

"Thank you." Provocateur accepts the card.

Savoie turns to Finley. "And the offer goes for you as well. Maybe we can work together in the future."

"Thank you." Finley stares at the card. "I'm actually planning a move to Los Angeles."

"Wonderful. Welcome to Hollywood! Give me a call when you're settled." Savoie looks over at Jason, who seems to be concentrating hard on the script. "And who can forget Che Guevara? Please, take one of my cards."

Jason looks up and half-smiles. "The name is actually Jason, but thanks."

"I'll be in touch, gentlemen." Savoie walks out.

"I consider this an excellent sign for our film." Provocateur beams with pride. "I am honored that you turned down a role to be my assassin, Finley."

"I had a vision in Death Valley..." Finley trails off, a bit embarrassed by his heat hallucination of Elvis.

Jason stares at this but says nothing.

Provocateur looks pensive. "Astonishing! You see, our success has been written on the scrolls of fate. We will reconvene Tuesday, but I encourage you to rehearse in the meantime."

Finley gathers his things and walks out of the conference room. He overhears Savoie finishing a story and Amy's genuine laughter.

Savoie stops talking to Amy when he sees Finley. "Finley! I've found myself in a bit of a jam. I wonder if you could help me out."

Finley clears his throat. "How can I be of service?"

"I took a taxi out here, but I really relish a chance to see Las Vegas again. Would you mind dropping me off at The Sands?"

"I can do that. It's just an old Mustang, though. I crack a window open when the air-conditioner misbehaves, and it's a stick shift."

"No problem. Desert air is a bit of a health tonic when you get to be my age."

They ride in silence for a few minutes, and Finley finds himself at a red light.

Savoie breaks the silence. "I want to be a producer on your movie, and I want a cameo."

"I think you're talking to the wrong person. I'm just an actor. And it's not exactly your kind of movie, from what I've heard about you." The light turns green, and Finley steps on the gas.

"But you have some influence on Provocateur. Although I can't figure out how or why. And you have some influence over Robbie Roberts."

"You make me sound like Machiavelli. I'm trying to make a life for myself, and I consider them friends. Do you know Robbie?"

Savoie exhales. "That's a long story, kid. Do you mind if I smoke?"

"I don't smoke, but I kind of like the smell."

"You know he's a drug addict, don't you?"

"That's really none of your business."

"You're defending him. That's good. Maybe it's none of my business, but I feel a little responsible. I got him started on the stuff, but I gave it up and he didn't."

"You should feel responsible. He almost died a few months ago. Did he work for you or something?"

"Something like that. It was a long time ago. What made you want to bring Marshmallow on Robbie's show in the first place? Your father made one appearance on the show, and it didn't go very well. It seems odd that you'd take the character back there."

"It's hard to explain. At first, I wanted a better interview for Marshmallow. I wanted to make things right. For Dad. And I did. Marshmallow was a hit. Then Robbie offered me a recurring role, and I needed a job. I wanted to be an actor, but *The Marshmallow Show* was what I knew, what I was used to. You know, my mother watched the show on repeat. I wasn't ready to let go. But I think Robbie helped me move on, and then I met Provocateur. It's all just really come together for me. As an actor."

Savoie doesn't respond right away, but he looks out the window for a few moments. "I see." Savoie remains silent for the rest of the trip, and Finley wonders if something upset his passenger.

Savoie says goodbye after the car stops in front of the casino.

Finley decides to call Robbie about the strange conversation. "Robbie? I just gave Jeff Savoie a ride to The Sands. Do you know him?"

"Yeah, I know that son of a bitch. Why?"

"He said he felt guilty about getting you hooked on drugs. I just wonder what he meant by that."

Robbie pauses for a moment before answering. "You and me both. We partied together back then, but I don't know why he'd say that. He's up to something, I don't know what. Maybe he's mad that I'm more relevant than he will ever be... Maybe steer clear of that guy. Don't pick up hitchhikers anymore, okay?"

"Yeah. He just showed up in Provocateur's office."

Robbie laughs. "Maybe he wants to do art films now. Who knows? I can't talk now, Finley. I'm on a date. Bye."

Mr. Sparkle and Scott feel enthusiastic about the impending trip to Spain, and they even ask Finley to invite Provocateur to a Spanish-themed dinner at the sprawling estate. To Finley's surprise, the enigmatic director accepts, and the hosts prepare a rare formal evening. Finley sits at the gleaming tablescape with a copy of *The Assassination of a Bullfighter*. He jots on a notepad with a ballpoint pen that he keeps behind an ear, a habit from college.

The maid, Imelda, sets the table with gold flatware and the gold-rimmed Mikasa salad plates, dinner plates, and soup bowls. Finley ducks out of her way whenever she sets something near him. Mr. Sparkle had considered a footman decked out in Spanish costume for the evening, but Scott declared the idea extravagant nonsense and insisted the funds go towards making the upcoming wedding more lavish.

Finley takes a break from the script to look at the printed menu for the evening. It begins with gazpacho and ends with a custard-crowned angel cake with fresh berries. He turns back to page 63 where his character has a crazed monologue at a chapel in Barcelona. As the bells toll, his character, Sebastian, becomes more aware of the impending assassination he must execute. Lost in thought at how to craft this performance, he's startled by Lee's barking at the doorbell signaling the arrival of Provocateur.

The director has gone to extremes, wearing a red suit and polka dot tie. He arrives with a baguette and an exotic potted orchid arrangement. The purple petals stand out in a deep jewel tone. "Good Evening." The director bows and clicks his heels in a crisp snap. Finley notices his python wingtips after the motion. The director asks, "Where is the bride-to-be?" He presents the bouquet of orchids.

Andrea comes out of the kitchen with mini bagels, each covered in various toppings. "Thanks for the flowers," she says. "Bagel?"

The director hands her the baguette and takes a bagel smattered with cream cheese and a brief fold of pink lox.

Cocktails have been set on bronze drinking tables. Finley coughs as he sips a concoction with too much vermouth. A mint leaf tops the drink. He doesn't know much about Spanish beverages, but he knows he'll never order this in Barcelona.

"Do you go to Spain often?" Andrea asks, her legs crossed, her hands holding a napkin under a mysterious pink drink.

Finley wonders if it's an homage to her favorite show, *Sex and the City*.

"Not as much as I would like. It's one of my favorite places after Las Vegas, Havana, and Berlin."

"I'm glad Finley's going to Barcelona instead of Berlin." She laughs. "I had a layover there and had to stay in the airport overnight. Someone kept singing in German, and it echoed everywhere. I couldn't get a wink of sleep."

"You should give Berlin another chance someday. Cities can surprise you with impermeable light." He stirs his old fashioned with a tiny straw.

"Isn't Paris the City of Light?" She lifts her eyebrow.

Finley cuts in before she can finish teasing Provocateur. "I've never been to Europe at all. Dad used to go to England sometimes, to Pinewood Studios with Marshmallow. He never took me." Finley trails off rather than continue the bitter memory.

"I'm jealous. You get to view Barcelona with new eyes. Europe will lavish you with its buffet of wonders. This will enhance your performance as Sebastian." Provocateur nods in satisfaction.

Finley notices Andrea stifling a giggle by sipping her drink through a tiny straw. He knows she views his friend as a pretentious hack, but Finley does feel that he's growing as an actor under Provocateur's direction.

Mr. Sparkle and Scott make their appearance, and everyone knows it's time to sit at the table. Finley remembers Mr. Sparkle saying, "Wasting calories on hors d'oeuvres is a deadly sin." Mr. Sparkle does look more slender tonight, dressed in a tight purple cummerbund.

Finley notices the gold cursive lettering on the name cards that sit before each place setting. He sits next to Andrea and Scott, across from Provocateur. Mr. Sparkle proudly sits at the head in a gold bamboo armchair. He's placed an ornamental candelabra in the shape of a calla lily in the center of the table.

Salad bowls seem to materialize on their own. Provocateur eyes the golden salad fork with suspicion, and Finley can't be sure that he likes the champagne vinaigrette framing pickled beets and arugula. He finds it a bit sour, but Scott made the dressing himself.

"If you need any help with the wedding reception, let me know. I'm happy that things worked out for this movie to happen. I've been fundraising for it before we finished *Fidelity*." Provocateur sips his wine.

"I've been planning every detail for a year." Andrea smiles. "I'm a bit of a control freak, let me tell ya."

Provocateur leans forward after a hiccup. "What do you think of Finley's costar, Jason?"

"I think he's balding. They get along alright?" Andrea swirls her unfinished cocktail, and Finley notices a smirk spreading over her face.

"Jason feels competitive with Finley. He thinks he should be the lead. I think this dynamic has an energy that I can use. If you've ever seen the movie *Ben-Hur*..."

"Can't say that I have." Andrea looks at a possible run in her stocking.

"Well, Charlton Heston was the lead actor. The director said nothing to him about his performance. Then, he told the other actor—nobody remembers his name—who was playing the bad guy, that his character made a pass at Ben-Hur and got rejected. That's why he tries to kill him with a chariot."

Andrea laughs. "Is there going to be a chariot race in the movie?"

Provocateur smiles. "I think Franco would have had his people die in chariot races if he could have gotten away with it. But I just wanted to tell you that Jason came to me on *Fidelity* to complain about Finley playing Fidel Castro."

"Really?" Finley asks.

"He said it was an instance of nepotism because of your father's famous bunny." The director watches his actor's reaction.

"Oh? And what did you say?"

"I said, of course it was, in the beginning. But Finley has something Charlton Heston had that makes him the lead. And Jason will never have that: It's called star quality. Jason is always going to lose the chariot race." He finishes with a flourish.

"Thank you. But I don't have a problem with nepotism. I deserve some kind of reward for growing up second banana to what Andrea calls 'that goddamn bunny.'" Finley fiddles with a crusty baguette and a pat of butter not quite easy to spread.

"Yeah, you do, baby." Andrea kisses him on the cheek.

"That's an enlightened view," Scott says from the end of the table.

"Is anyone ready for dessert? Individual angel cakes with various fruits and whipped cream in a dessert glass," Mr. Sparkle offers.

"Very light. Like a fluffy cloud," Scott advertises.

"Yes, we celebrate with sweets because we're going to Spain!" Provocateur stands up with his wine. "I'd like to toast to Finley and Andrea. May they have years of happiness."

They drink to that, but Finley notices Scott and Mr. Sparkle moving to the grand piano. He wonders if Mr. Sparkle will talk-sing his way around a lounge song while Scott does his best to make his spouse shine with perfect piano playing. He's surprised to see Mr. Sparkle sit on a velvet sofa while Scott takes a seat alone at the piano. He hears Scott begin a Rachmaninoff concerto with surprising virtuosity. He wonders if the couple has reached some sort of detente, and Mr. Sparkle is sharing the spotlight for once.

Finley walks over to the gold sideboard and picks up his second angel cake parfait. The dry-textured cake disappoints, but the whipped cream saves the day. He watches Andrea listening to the classical piece and notices how her face softens out of its usual wary look. He makes a mental note that classical music might calm her during their occasional arguments.

Scott finishes the song, and the small group applauds. He starts his next number, and Finley notices the familiar chords of an Elton John song, "Benny and the Jets." Andrea rushes to the piano room and takes off her pink Versace La Medusa heels. She goes into a practiced dance routine with barrel turns and a stagger step that lines up with the stuttered chorus. Her energy surprises him as much as Scott's perfect pitch. This must be a special song for the family.

The dinner guest, Provocateur, seems to find the performance less impressive. He looks at his rectangular Cartier watch and yawns. As Andrea lands her last stagger step, Provocateur shakes hands with Mr. Sparkle and approaches Finley to say goodbye.

"I'll see you at the wedding and in Barcelona, if not before then. Work on centering and meditation in the meantime. Study up on the script and create your take on the character, but I don't have to tell you that, do I? I know you'll bring the same level of professionalism as you did for Fidel." He shakes Finley's hand, but Finley gives him a hug instead.

Provocateur says a more formal goodbye to Andrea, who has a slight grin on her face.

Delicious night, Finley thinks.

The next morning, a mild autumn Saturday, Finley yawns and saunters through the long hallway to the mirrored dining room. He pours himself coffee and grabs and cheese Danish off the gold platter as usual, and nods at Scott, who wears a quilted green robe. He looks up as he bites into his Danish and notices his fiancée seated across from him. Most Saturday mornings find Andrea Rizzo in her office at The Laga Brutto, but she has changed her schedule.

"Let's talk." Andrea sips Lady Grey tea from a floral teacup on a matching saucer.

"Yes, dear." He stretches and yawns. "Is this about the wedding or Spain? Or how you long to tell Provocateur that his brand of pretentious filmmaking is all wrong?" Finley grins at her.

"It's about after the wedding."

"Oh?"

"With all due respect to my stepfather here, I wanted to get your thoughts on our living situation. I ran into Robbie Roberts the other day, and he's looking up old connections in Los Angeles. He's worried about the future, and he got me thinking about mine. And I know you know that I'm not Provocateur's biggest fan, but the film industry is in LA. And your career is tied up with both these guys, and it's all pointing to Los Angelas. And I do believe in you."

"We've talked about this. Are you saying we should move now?" He stares at her for a minute.

"Yes. I'm not going to abandon Sparkle, Inc.. But Dad's retired. I think we have enough earnings on royalties from our back catalog, including *The Marshmallow Show*, to keep afloat even if I'm not in Las Vegas. It was great living here when I was single..."

"So...house hunting in L.A.? How will we afford that? I don't think we'll be moving anytime soon with the housing shortage over there." Finley laments the bleak prospect of expensive real estate.

Scott clears his throat and puts down his newspaper. "You know, when I was a younger man, I had a bit of an acting career in Los Angeles."

"I saw your headshot from *Young Sherlock Holmes*! In Glenda's office," Finley remembers.

"I was also a drug dealer in a surfing movie with Gary Busey, *New Waves*. And some stage work. I was almost in the L.A. production of *Cats*, you know. I was *this* close to being Skimbleshanks. Then they brought in the actor from the London production, just like what happened with Zero Mostel and the movie version of *Fiddler*. But my point is, I also invested in real estate before I met Chas."

"You mean that 1937 cottage-style bungalow? With the cream brick fireplace and the stained-glass window?" Andrea asks with growing excitement. "And the spiral staircase that goes up to a split-level second floor with a total of 1800 square feet? And the metal kitchen cabinets that were popular in the '50s and put in after the second owner remodeled it?"

"Yes. I see you remember the place. Technically, I still own it. We use it sometimes instead of staying in a hotel if we need to get over there, but I don't see why I couldn't rent it out to the right couple who want to make a new start."

"You're the best dad in the world!" Andrea hugs Scott.

"I don't know if I can give up breakfast here," Finley says. "But I can't turn a good bungalow down. If it meets my specifications. Does it have a swimming pool?" He's really gotten used to having a pool, but he's only teasing her.

"Actually, it does. But you'll have to give up a tennis court in the move." Andrea puts jelly on an English muffin and sips her tea.

"When do I get a tour?" Finley asks. He remembers his calendar stands empty today. "What do you say, Scott? You made the offer."

"We'd better hurry up if we're going to miss lunch traffic. We're taking my blue Chevy, by the way. The convertible."

"I'm dressed. I'll just throw on a red scarf and a big hat...like *Pretty Woman*." Andrea happens to be wearing a cheetah-print jumpsuit.

"I'm not going shopping on Rodeo Drive. You're not marrying Richard Gere." Finley starts to feel waves of dread at the prospect of shopping; he imagines snooty old ladies looking at him with critical eyes. Even worse, he fears that no one will want his autograph or recognize him from *Fidelity*.

"We'll see. Scott's in charge today. I think I'll make the stars on Rodeo Drive say, 'Julia who?' in this outfit!" Andrea struts like she's on a catwalk, and Finley laughs.

"Don't forget who the real movie star is," Finley says in a mock-serious tone.

"I think that would be me. Remember *New Waves*. And *Sherlock Holmes*. It's elementary, my dear," Scott chimes in and pantomimes smoking a pipe.

"Hollywood, here we come. But we have to get going to tour the bungalow of the stars. Road trip!" Andrea rushes to pack a tote bag and find her Versace sunglasses.

"Does Chas want to come with?" Finley turns to Scott.

"He's...not feeling well." Scott looks towards the bedroom. "He's still recovering from the dinner party. Chas isn't a spring chicken, you know."

Finley can see something in Scott's face that makes him want to change the subject and he guesses that the subject is Lorraine. He knows Lorraine plans to attend the wedding and there's some sort of drama between Chas, Scott, and Andrea's mother, but he doesn't want to pry. "I'll fill the cooler up for the trip."

"Don't you dare bring Cheetos or Bugles. White leather interior, Finley!"

"Fanta? Perrier?"

"Don't push it. More Perrier than Fanta. And we still have those watercress sandwiches from Tuesday's lunch."

"Those are yours. I'll make peanut butter and jelly. Maybe Andrea will eat an orange at least."

Andrea comes out of the bedroom with an enormous tote and gigantic sunglasses to match. A red scarf holds a wide-brimmed hat in place. "Why don't you sit in the back with the cooler, Finley? I'm navigating for Scott."

"Really? More sandwiches for me. I brought a Moby CD."

Scott groans, "We can compromise. Paul Anka after Moby."

On the road at last, Finley drinks a bottle of Fanta in the spacious leather backseat. The wind blows Andrea's giant map around, and he can barely hear Moby's techno beats, but Scott loves having the top of the convertible down. Palm tree after palm tree gives way to desert as they leave Las Vegas. Los Angelas seems so close but also worlds away. He calls Robbie on his cell phone, "Where are you?"

"I'm sitting at an olive wood desk at a Burbank studio."

"What are you doing in Los Angeles?" Finley's surprised Robbie is nearby.

"I'm putting feelers out with some old connections. If my producer comes down for a visit, like I've heard, it's very bad. Kiss of death. From an anaconda with vampire fangs. I need an escape route if the ship goes down with the whole enchilada."

"We'll be in Los Angeles. Scott, Andrea, and me. We're taking a tour of a bungalow."

"Call me back at 5. I'm busy right now. Maybe we can get cocktails when you get here."

"Right."

"And even if you move here, you're still recurring, Finley. And don't even think about jumping ship. The bunny's name is Marshmallow, and she stays with me."

"Okay, Robbie. But I'm a movie star now, so you're lucky to have me on the show."

"Right, kid. Don't quit your day job."

"Asshole."

"Son of a bitch. See you soon. If you're done at the bungalow before 6, I'll give you a tour of this place."

"Where are you?"

"I'm on the old Universal Creative Artists lot."

"Wow. I've always wanted to see that place. Text me directions."

"You just make a left at the cigar lounge on Sunset Boulevard and a right at the spot where Grauman's Chinese Theatre used to be, and another left at the spot where the Brown Derby used to be..."

"Umm...I think we'll just use the map."

"Suit yourself."

Finley soon finds himself falling asleep, despite or because of the rushing, dry wind through the windows and the warm leather around him. He notices the car has slowed, and they seem to be off the highway and on residential roads. His body resists waking up, although his eyelids flutter at the changing sunlight and shade in the neighborhood.

"We're here!" Scott says, and Finley opens his eyes.

Between two majestic palm trees sits a cottage-style bungalow. Its historic marker emblazoned with **1937** in bronze. Its lawn stands in manicured glory. An enormous cupid planter on the porch sports a miniature orange tree. They exit the Chevy, and Finley walks behind Andrea, holding her hand. A hush comes over the couple as they let the house work its magic over them. Scott fishes out a hidden key in the stone cupid's mouth and opens the door to a tasteful foyer. Finley notices a red Coupe de Ville parked to the side of the driveway, and whispers to Scott, "Is anyone else here?"

"I called some friends in real estate to give you a proper tour. They really love the history of the era. I think they're having a snack in the kitchen. I told them to bring a charcuterie board and wine."

"Wow, you went all out. Thanks." Finley is almost speechless.

After looking into a compact living room with tufted, white sofas and the famous cream fireplace, they make their way into the little French kitchen, admiring the stone backsplash and porcelain 1930s sink. Finley notices a spiral staircase behind some boxes in the little den beside the dining room; he doesn't know where the staircase goes, but it doesn't seem anyone's climbed it in years.

"Scott, you didn't tell me your daughter was drop-dead gorgeous!" A redhead dressed in a filmy tropical tunic stands up from a glass table and embraces Scott. She turns to Andrea and gives her a broad hug. "I don't know if you remember me. I'm Jan. I used to babysit you at my house in Encino. You might remember a certain lop-eared bunny."

"I do. I think it peed on me, and you gave me a clean shirt and an ice cream sandwich as bribes. Thank you for meeting us here, and I can't wait to hear the whole spiel." Andrea's eyes take in every possible detail of the kitchen. She stares at a beautiful French chandelier in the dining room beyond, far more interested in touring the house than catching up with Jan.

"I want to hear more about this bunny," Finley says. He really doesn't know too much about Andrea's childhood.

"I'll tell you the whole story someday." Jan laughs with a glance at Andrea.

Andrea glares a bit but not too much.

The man at the table, who bears an uncanny resemblance to a young Anthony Perkins, stands up as well. Finley notices the white carnation in his boutonniere and the immaculate polka dot tie and white shirt. "Neil Green, real estate guru at large. Here's my business card if you ever decide to upgrade from this fabulous bungalow. We could have a bit of charcuterie and wine before we dive into the tour," he suggests.

Finley looks at the gold-lettered cursive on the business card. The N stands out, an enormous overstatement, and glided vines make an ornate border. The name, **Glorious**

Hollywood Homes, proclaims itself like an exclamation point in a different font. "Why don't we let Jan and Andrea get a head start? Split up the tour. I could really use some ham and cheese." Finley can see his fiancée's eyes gleaming at the possibilities of a new home. He knows he can't stop Andrea once she gets an idea.

Finley wolfs down his seventh slice of peppered Genoa ham and provolone on an artisan cracker while Neil waits to have a chat. Neil sips some Chardonnay. After feeling less hungry, Finley remembers his manners. "Do you have any interesting stories about the house?" Finley can't think of anything else to say because the house seems fine as far as he's concerned.

"I've heard that George Raft may have entertained Al Capone in the dining room with beverages and ladies of the night, but it's never been verified." Neil has a slight grin on his face. "I do want to point out something without alarming Andrea. I saw a mouse in the corner of the dining room. I'd recommend an exterminator before you move in. You don't want any...unwelcome surprises awaiting you."

"Thanks for letting me know. I'll tell Scott. He's my landlord now. We'll get rid of that mouse and any friends he might have around." Finley lowers his voice. "Does the house have any other problems I need to know about?"

"Well, you might want to get that A/C looked at, and maybe a roofer could clean up there a bit. I'd change the countertops to marble and update the cabinets, but that's me. I think if you get a good professional cleaning after the exterminator comes in, it's move-in ready."

"Awesome." Finley loads another cracker with a double-decker of ham and cheese.

"You know, I heard that you're an actor. I happen to be an aspiring filmmaker myself. I want to make films that mean something—about how one powerful man can change an evil world. I'm polishing a script about a man who's really an angel living in the desert. He desperately wants to save humankind but can't find the goodness in people." Neil Green's eyes light with zeal as he talks about the script.

"That sounds very...dramatic. Who did you have in mind for the role of the angel?"

"Well, it's a role that I'm tailoring for myself. I'd be writing and directing. I think of myself as a burgeoning auteur director, the next Orson Welles. But I'd love to know what you think of the script. Would you mind if I sent a copy to your address? It's about 400 pages, single-spaced. I really want to focus on the angel's disintegrating faith in the role of humans. And I'd welcome any feedback. I tend to go off on tangents like a satellite that's spinning out of orbit. Maybe I just need a voice of reason to reel me back in." Neil laughs in a nervous manner.

"I wouldn't say I'm the voice of reason, but I'm really curious about your script. Sure." Finley doesn't know what to say. Maybe he could pass the script onto Provocateur.

"I'm just worried that I'd be courting controversy with the conservative portions of the audience." Neil gulps his chardonnay. "You see, the angel is a fully realized sexual being."

"Umm...yeah. Could be controversial. You know, I feel like I'm missing the tour. I mean, I'm going to live here, you know? Thanks for telling me about...about the mouse, and we'll talk when I get a look at that script." Finley doesn't want to stick around to hear any sexual aspects of Neil's character and gets up to find Andrea, Scott, and Jan.

"I'll catch up when I finish this Chardonnay. It's a crime to waste a good bottle of wine," Neil responds, but Finley has already rushed into the living room. "Suit yourself," Neil hiccups and pours another glass.

"...and the crown molding around the windows dates back to the original 1937 architecture." Jan points at an elaborate bay window at the end of the living room. "The window seat, however, was a later addition."

Andrea grasps his hand. "Finley, we're getting a window seat! Where's Neil?"

"He's finishing up all the wine for us. He wants to send me a copy of the script he's writing, but it seems kind of scary, even by Provocateur's standards."

"Welcome to L.A., Finley. Every waitress or barista has a script they're working on, and everyone swears they are the next Spielberg." Andrea laughs.

Ring-a-ding-ding!

A week before the wedding, Finley wakes to Robbie and John standing over him. Did Scott actually let them inside the house? He stretches and yawns.

"Rise and shine! It's your buck's night!" says Tuckman.

"What?" Finley rubs his eyes and puts on a shirt.

"He means your bachelor party! We're taking you to a mystery destination, but we'll have you back Monday. Pack your rubbers and blow." Robbie starts opening Finley's dresser drawers.

"What? Huh?" Finley looks up from the sock drawer.

"Don't worry. Your party planner has everything squared. Can you pack in 20 minutes? We can't miss this." Robbie picks up a tote bag near the dresser.

"What about coffee? And my cheese Danish? And a shower?"

"You might want to wait on that. There's coffee where we're going, and you'll NEED a shower tomorrow."

"We're not going to Tijuana or something? I'm really not into donkey shows." Finley hopes Robbie hasn't planned something weird.

"We're in the buck's night capital of the world, mate! And definitely no donkeys, but there will be some ass." Tuckman sounds certain of this.

"Showgirls?" Finley wonders.

"Oh, we'll start there. The night begins with feathers and class and ends with the birds who dance with their ass. I just wrote that, by the way." Robbie looks pleased with his poem.

"And you can quote him. But, if you don't mind, you've got to get in the vehicle blindfolded. Can't have you peeking." Tuckman takes out the blindfold and moves towards Finley.

"Okay... Let me get dressed first." He grabs a Hawaiian button-down and some dark jeans. "Can I have some privacy?" He wants his friends out of his room.

"Okay, but I'm going to get you blindfolded and in the limo. It's my job as a best man," Robbie calls while walking out of the bedroom.

Getting in what he believes might be a stretch limo, he senses more people than just Robbie and John.

"Finally! We can go. I've almost finished all the champagne on this side."

"Provocateur?"

"Are you ready for the ultimate ritual of the toxic bourgeois male?"

"Yes?" Finley hesitates, his blindfold chafing a bit as they head towards the mystery destination.

Provocateur lets out a guttural party-scream.

"Calm on down now," Finley hears a familiar voice responding to Provocateur. It's a Nashville accent, something he hasn't heard in a while. He thinks for a moment, then realizes it must be his best friend, Jeremy.

"Jeremy? Is that you?" He can't believe Robbie located his best friend from high school, but Finley remembers a suspicious conversation a few weeks ago when Robbie asked him personal details about his life before he moved to California and then Vegas. He didn't realize it was for party planning. Robbie could be very sly at times.

"I'm right here, Finley. Did you think I would miss your bachelor party? I'm a groomsman, should have been the best man, but I'll save that discussion for later. It's about time you gave up on that bunny and started paying attention to real women. I think Robbie has set the wheels in motion."

Someone places a glass in Finley's hand, and he drinks a cocktail somewhere between absinthe and champagne. The ice-cold liquid hits his throat, and the taste spreads across his tongue. "That's what Tuckman calls a 'steadier' but I'm not sure this Australian guy knows what he's talking about. Says he's a chef or something."

"Why don't you try one, Jeremy?" Tuckman replies, undaunted.

"Whoa, that kicks like a mule. I stand corrected," Jeremy concedes. "And don't worry, Finley. I know you've missed out on my singing career in Nashville, but I want to thank you for supporting me. I want to thank the Las Vegas community for its friendliness to my music career. I've lined up a few gigs, but I'm not going to miss that wedding of yours. I brought my guitar, and I'll play some good country music until we get to our destination. I'm calling it, 'The Bachelor Party Song.'" Jeremy strums a few bars on his acoustic guitar:

"We're riding into the night.
We found ourselves a limousine.
Drinking in the backseat,
I think the liquor turned green.
I don't know these guys,
But Finley seems to like them.
So, I'll just stay awhile,
And get to know the women.
Las Vegas guys' night.
It's going on past midnight.
Bachelor party, alright,
It's Finley's wild night."

The limousine pulls into a parking spot, and Finley can't tell how far they've gone. His friends help him out and guide him through the door. "Can I take off the blindfold? It's itchy," Finley complains.

"Hold your horses. We're almost there," Jeremy answers.

Still blindfolded, Finley gets blasted by Vegas air-conditioning. He's in a hotel-casino, but which one? He hears the rushing water of a large fountain. As they continue walking, he hears more rushing water. The air seems cool, and he can feel that the floor has a smooth, glassy texture beneath his feet. After an elevator ride, Robbie takes off the blindfold. Finley notices his friend Jeremy Berry hasn't changed too much since last he saw him, except now Jeremy has a deep tan and large cowboy hat. His friend looks amazed by the sights, and Finley can't help looking around himself.

Finley realizes he must be in the hotel-casino known as The Realm of Venus. The place had become notorious for allowing female guests to go topless in several areas of the resort, particularly The Temple of Love Casino. Mosaic walls depicting the goddess in various incarnations surround the ballroom. Red urns sporting Romanesque figures in black paint, set in enormous nooks carved into walls, tower towards the domed ceilings. The rich reds of the mosaic contrast with the gold chandelier, the grand focal point of the ballroom. Statues of Venus and a male discus-thrower flank the entrance of the party room. Finley sees statues of other mythical figures of Roman mythology, but he doesn't know enough of the mythos to identify them all.

Finley sees guests in togas milling about the fantastical, Roman-styled ballroom. A man with a laurel crown over his pate feeds grapes to a young woman by tossing them in her mouth from across the table. A red-haired woman lies on a chaise as men in togas fan her with peacock feathers. Her open toga reveals most of her body rather than covering it.

"The Realm of Venus? I've heard about this place."

Robbie spreads his arms wide at the expanse before them. "This is not The Realm of Venus. Not as ordinary guys know it. This is the hidden world of the Vegas private party. This is Robbie Robert's Realm, and I'm giving you, a mere mortal, a glimpse into the debauchery of Emperors. Let's get those togas on!"

Finley can't resist heading to a large window with a spectacular view of the Las Vegas Strip. The scale of the city impresses him. Somehow, a magical city of electric light towers high into the desert air, surrounded by palm trees. Tonight, all of it belongs to him, or at least he can imagine it does at this party.

A man with extraordinarily defined shoulders scowls nearby in a toga. He's drinking with an extraordinarily bosomed blonde. He nods to Robbie.

"I'll be right back. Get your freak on!" Robbie raises his glass of Prosecco and drinks all the liquid at once. Robbie walks over to join his guest by a decorated mosaic window. The blonde woman excuses herself in a hurry, eager to get away from the man.

"Hope you're enjoying yourself, Yuri."

"We have business." Yuri's voice crackles in a low bass.

"This is a bachelor party. Nothing more sacred in Vegas. Business waits. Try to have fun."

"I can't promise anything. But I got party favors. This is my idea of fun."

Robbie smiles and accepts an envelope. "My kind of business."

"We talk later, Robbie." Yuri scans the ballroom with narrowed eyes and moves towards a group of entertainers.

The giant cake must be unveiled to kick off the night. This masterwork of a hardworking Vegas baker stands: a rude, glistening pair of pointy breasts, tall at a full five feet and marvelously wider in circumference. The frosting is delicious, but the cake is quite hollow. Each nipple boasts a lit taper.

"Blow out the nipples, Finley. Make a wish." Robbie beams with pride at the lurid confection.

Finley blows out the candles as a crowd of men sing "For He's a Jolly Good Fellow." Jeremy's Nashville baritone voice stands out among the crowd.

Suddenly, the cake begins to jiggle and out pops a leggy lady dressed in little more than a cherry on top. It takes a moment, but Finley recognizes the notorious tennis star, Gabi Masters, more widely known for her nude photos and scandals than her brief tennis career. He'd mentioned to Robbie that he'd had a crush on the star.

Now, here she is, tan, blonde, toned, and ready to dance on his lap. Finley holds his lap very still—to move even an inch would be infidelity to Andrea, given his arousal. He can see the glitter in her blonde hair, those lovely green eyes gazing at him without the violent rage she usually displays during televised tennis matches. Her stiletto heels occasionally graze his knee, but she makes it through the disco song without disaster. She moves like a fantasy.

Fantasies invariably end, and she kisses him on the cheek. "Congratulations on your wedding!" Her Cooperstown, New York, accent looms as large in person as on television.

Finley overhears raised voices and excuses himself to investigate. But he goes back to the party after a brief glance; Robbie can handle himself, after all.

A manager arrives on the scene. "Your Russian friend is making the girls uncomfortable."

"He's Ukrainian," Robbie says, swigging something from a flask.

"Who cares about geography? He needs to stop. He comes up to one of my employees and says, 'You are prostitute, no?' They don't like that word. I can get you escorts if that's what you want. But The Realm of Venus, we got standards. This is a classy operation."

"I'll talk to him. It's a cultural misunderstanding." Robbie nods, trying to appear understanding.

"You better talk to him. Next time, he's out of here. Have fun, but keep my employees happy, okay?" He pats Robbie on the shoulder.

"I'll talk to Yuri. Thanks for the party! The groom is having the time of his life!" Robbie pulls a few hundred-dollar bills from his wallet. "Give this to the ladies for their troubles."

The manager smiles, crinkling his leathery face. "Enjoy yourself, Mr. Roberts."

"I always do." Robbie walks away with quick steps; he needs to find Yuri before he causes more trouble. He stops right before he gets to him. He's too late. Finley's cowboy friend has grabbed Yuri by the shirt. A blonde woman in skimpy attire sits with tears in her eyes.

"Someone needs to teach you a lesson! That's no way to speak to a lady."

"She is no lady. She is a prostitute." Yuri sticks out his chin as he repeats the word, then spits in Jeremy's face.

Enraged, Jeremy hits him on his nose.

Yuri falls on the floor and stares at Robbie a moment. He picks himself up and runs straight out the door. Some problems, reflects Robbie, have a way of working themselves out.

Finley, watching a stripper effortlessly glide down a pole to jazz and shaking her silver heels at the bottom, is having a ball. But three old fashioneds haven't mixed well with the limo drinks. He can feel something like heartburn and nausea rising in his chest, thinking about all the cocktails he's just imbibed. He tries to belch but throws up all over the mirrored bar.

The bartender prepares rags and a mop, and he is the last sight Finley sees before tumbling off the swivel stool. He puts out his hand in time but slides on his own vomit.

The party's over.

Finley wakes up, mostly clean, in a complimentary Realm of Venus room. A plaque reads, **The Italian Stallion Suite.** He feels something on his shoulder and sees the guys must have taken an ordinary Marshmallow Bunny doll and dressed her in lingerie: red thong and sequined bra. They've even added ridiculous sequined lips. She's wearing a sign that says, **Fuck me**.

They thought of everything...except aspirin, coffee, and a cheese Danish.

Robbie's doing everything he can to stay out of rehab. He's even buying groceries for himself. How many bottles of cold medicine can he buy without raising eyebrows? The drowsy kind. If he can drug himself into a stupor, the temptation for illegal drugs will fade. It's a healthy way, right? He's switched to beer on weekdays.

He sees Yuri, unnaturally relaxed, smoking outside the store on a picnic table.

"Get me a prostitute," whispers Yuri.

"Keep it down! You need to take that word out of your vocabulary. You almost got kicked out of The Realm of Venus! At least be discreet, asshole."

"Why are you buying this NyQuil? You have a cold?"

"I'm stocking up for flu season," Robbie lies.

"I am not an asshole. I want to make love with a nice lady, any lady. I am being honest."

"I'm just stocking up for flu season. Maybe get a nice suit, and the ladies will follow. Manners, hygiene, asshole."

"If I get a suit and stop saying 'prostitute,' can I be a camera grip on the show? Mother's business is slower."

"Sure, kid. Sure. Just show up tomorrow morning? You can start in the props department and work your way up."

"I want to attend Finley's wedding. Mother is going with you. I'm your plus two. I can meet a nice lady there in a suit."

"Are you in a suit or is the lady? I think that's a dangling participle. Just don't say that word we talked about. But I guess I'll ask Finley if you can go. Why not?"

"What is this dangling? Something dirty?"

"Never mind, Yuri. Never mind." Robbie suspects Yuri wouldn't be interested in grammatical discussions.

Yuri stands still for a moment, and Robbie gets an uneasy feeling and looks around.

Robbie notices two guys approaching him. He recognizes drug dealers from the Strip. "Hey, are you looking to do business?" Robbie perks up a bit. He's a bit concerned, however, when Yuri suddenly flees the scene. Yuri doesn't stop running until he's out of the parking lot.

"You didn't pay us last time. We went to your place, and you didn't show." The red-haired thug stretches his neck and cracks his knuckles. The thug with the acne scars and woolen hat suddenly punches Robbie in the jaw.

The other one, pale as a vampire with slicked-back red hair, looks a bit sympathetic.

Robbie steps back, rubbing his cheek. "Hey! I think you cracked one of my teeth! Son of a bitch. I'm good for it. It's not my fault I was in rehab when you came over. So...you got some blood on you?" Robbie can't help smiling a little before he says the next part.

"No shit."

"Gee, you might want to get tested for HIV now. I'm just raising awareness here out of 'kindness.' I'm HIV-positive."

Their mouths fall open, but neither moves or speaks.

"I guess I'll be taking my business elsewhere, but golly, I hope you accept this payment." Robbie peels bills off one by one to the floor. He's making it rain. Out of the corner of his eye as he walks away, he sees the thugs diving for the cash. He starts whistling, some jazz tune Gouda's cooking up. Getting clean is cancelled for the day; Robbie heads to the Strip for a fix. He might even treat himself to a speedball.

He finds his friend under the same old bridge as last time.

She looks vacant and one eye stays closed. Her condition seems much improved since last time.

"Won't you make a guest appearance on the show for old times' sake?" He tries to encourage the former star as he sits on the folded newspapers beside her.

Vera shakes her head. "I've lost my looks. The sharks'll tear me to pieces."

"You've still got it. Give me that face from your famous closeup."

She squints and pops the good eye out a bit, a garish parody of her old face. In the movie, she'd been a beautiful, wronged lover draped in a mink stole. Now, she resembles that woman haggard and worn.

Robbie tries to hide his real feelings and gets down to business. "Speedball?"

"I got a spoon and a lighter, babe. Donations accepted." She taps the spoon against her cheek and smiles with her lips tight against her cheeks, eyes unblinking.

Robbie shudders at her unnatural visage but accepts the spoon nonetheless.

After the speedballs, they lean against the brick wall, gazing at the flames of Vera's makeshift firepit. Robbie puts his arm around the former actress. The high makes watching fire a visceral experience. Robbie sees fire-zebras kicking up their back legs and wearing feathery hats. He's not sure what Vera sees; one eye stares as her ragged breathing continues. The other eye remains closed. Hours go by with distorted speed, and they both fall asleep just before the Vegas sunrise.

"I thought you'd reached the nadir of sleaze, but you continue to surprise me," he hears a voice above him say.

Robbie wakes up to find Vera gone and a vaguely familiar young man standing over him. The glare in his eyes is as disconcerting as the desert sun. Robbie shields his face and blinks. "Where's Vera?" He yawns and rubs his eyes.

"I took my mother home, and I'll give you ten minutes to wake up and walk away before I call the police. You didn't give her drugs, but you sure didn't stop her. You really are a worm, Robbie."

"I had a bad day. Thanks for looking out for Vera."

"Nine minutes now." The man points at his silver watch.

"Okay, I'm walking, I'm walking!" Instead of walking to his condominium, Robbie heads to Fremont Street and ends up at The Silver Rush. Music soothes the soul; he knows Gouda and The Stuffed Hams practice on Wednesday.

He sits in the front row of the auditorium with his feet on the chrome bar in front. "Play something from that album you did years ago. You know, 'Rain Gets in Your Trumpet.'"

Gouda nods, and Mr. Prosciutto heads to the mic. Mr. Prosciutto straightens a white satin tie with a sequined saxophone on it. The tie matches his pinstripe pants in spirit, if not in fact.

"*Music soothes the soul in pain,*
Even walking home in the rain."

Robbie notices Yuri lurking around the studio with an expression a lost dog might have. He's never seen him without the perpetual hostility. He almost feels Yuri might be a human being, but a human being might have had the sense of decency not to invade Robbie's privacy. Robbie avoids any sign that he even sees the younger man.

Yuri sits next to him anyway on the fading row of red theater chairs. "I'm sorry." Yuri shrugs.

"Did you tell them where I would be and stall me?" Robbie whispers.

"I didn't know they would beat you." Yuri lifts his chin and looks him straight in the eye.

"Did you think they were going to bake me a cake?" Robbie lets the question hang in the air.

"You let the man in the cowboy hat hit me at The Realm of Venus. You said nothing." Yuri feels he has made a valid point.

"Nobody invited you in the first place. Look, I appreciated the party favors, but the manager was ready to throw you out. I stood up for you. But then, you made a woman cry. Your actions had consequences." Robbie wants him to understand.

Silence. Yuri averts his gaze.

Robbie moves to another seat, turns his attention to The Stuffed Hams.

Yuri eventually leaves The Silver Rush; Robbie knows he'll never see him again.

Robbie has been putting off his next visit to Olga's office, but he's out of all his drugs and can't fathom doing his next episode without them. He needs something to calm his nerves after being hit, and she owes him that because Yuri sold him out.

He's surprised to see a strange man at the reception desk. He simply nods Robbie into Olga's office. The guy already seems an improvement over Yuri, as far as Robbie is concerned.

"Robbie!" Olga embraces him, squeezing his kidneys in the process. "Yuri's been arrested. He was with a sex-worker during a hotel raid."

"You mean a prostitute," Robbie quips.

Out of one side of her mouth while lighting a cigarette, Olga says, "That word should never be used in front of a woman. It's now considered as rude as the word 'whore.'

That's something Yuri needs to learn before he gets into more trouble."

"Okay, sex-worker. Doesn't have the same poetic ring as 'whore' in my opinion, but what do I know? Which hotel?" That's about all he wants to know.

"It was a room at New Jersey, New Jersey. Please, Robbie. Bail him out." Olga pleads, placing her hands around his neck in an embrace.

"Are you kidding me? That son of bitch caused trouble at Finley's bachelor party AND he got me beat up. You know I'm crazy about you, but your son has gotten on my bad side." He smiles at her, knowing she's going to get her way.

"I'll send him back to Kiev! My father can teach him to behave if anyone can. I promise you, he's gone, if you bail him out. But I can't send him to Kiev if he's in jail."

"Yuri being a continent away? Now that's a public service. I'll do it for Las Vegas. I'll do it for you. Not for him. And I want him gone at least a year...or three." He looks her straight in the eyes.

Tears form around Olga's false eyelashes and her foundation runs a little in the small crinkles at the corners of her eyes. "Yes. Yes. You don't have to worry about him anymore. You understand he's my only son? I've spoiled him, and I ignored his failings."

"Well, let's get down to cases. I'd like a few refills, Doctor." He sits on a swivel chair and puts his feet up on a gold coffee table.

"Robbie...your nose is bleeding. You've got to go easy on this stuff." Olga's eyebrows rise with concern.

Robbie steals tissues from Olga's desk and inserts them in his nose. "Can you give me that combo injection again? Steroids and B12? Please?" He holds her hands and stares into her eyes.

"Yes, yes. Roll up the sleeve and squeeze this little ball." She knows his veins very well after years of practice.

"Yes, Doctor. But then I want my lollipops."

She gives him two injections, and he starts to perk up. "Liquid energy. Youth in a syringe. You're a miracle-worker!" Robbie gives her a kiss.

Olga sits at the glossy desk. She's already signing the scripts for the legal prescriptions. She hands him several blue envelopes as well.

Robbie grins like a kid in a candy store and walks out whistling. He turns around in the doorway like he's forgotten something. "Are you busy? Why don't we check into our place, and I can get you dinner tonight?"

"I should take advantage of your state after my injections."

"I want to reciprocate with an injection of my own, baby."

"I'll tell Maximo to cancel my appointments. But I want to change first and wear a necklace and something with sequins. Like a lady. I'll meet you. Have champagne on ice. Something cheap and sweet, not that dry shit."

"You got it." He kisses her with too much tongue because she loves it that way and leaves.

Robbie's joy over reconciliation with Olga sustains him for a bit, as do the contents of the various envelopes, but a memo on his desk from Ms. Wise sends him reeling again. He'd just noticed it after arriving for rehearsal for the talk show. Michelle Wise is the producer of *Robbie Roberts Tonight!* in the sense that her name appears in the credits. She'd taken a stand-off approach ever since the show fell into a steady pattern of rehearsal and content, and she seemed happy enough to give Robbie creative control. A visit from Michelle Wise happened as often as a shooting star, a memo even rarer.

Robbie sits in the gray modern office and takes a deep breath before opening the envelope. He feels relief tinged with terror, like a patient about to be jabbed with a needle after hours of waiting. He opens it and reads the thing after several attempts at meditation.

Robbie,

You're family to me. Robbie Roberts Tonight! is a jewel in my crown. And you protect something precious, am I right? I've heard some rumors through the grapevine about your personal problems. I'm not going to pry. But we're family. A family keeps things functioning. A family supports its members. I'm like your Jewish mother. Let's keep a great thing going. Let's have a talk. Meet me at 4:00 today for Happy Hour at The Refreshments of Venus. Our usual booth. Order me a pink martini or whatever is trendy right now.

With great warmth and sincerity,
Michelle Wise.

Robbie digs in his desk for that wonder drug of an anti-anxiety pill. He misses the good old days when you could get Valium if you needed it. Not even Olga can get him that; he'd tried but nobody manufactures the name brand anymore.

He can't listen to Gouda's band without thinking about the upcoming meeting, can't concentrate on the week's script, so he shows up early to The Refreshments of Venus.

The hostess smooths her toga and adjusts her olive wreath before she notices Robbie waiting for a table.

"I'm here for the most important meeting of my life. Can you please get me the booth next to the cascading waterfall?"

He sees her hesitate, and he puts a one-hundred-dollar bill in her hand.

"Of course, Mr. Roberts."

Hours later, Robbie nurses his second old-fashioned and bites a mass of calamari that succeeds only in not being chewy. He's focused on the seafood and doesn't notice Michelle sitting down across from him.

The red-haired bartender does notice and puts a special Caligula's Cosmo in front of her that Robbie ordered in advance. Robbie stares for a moment; Michelle's signature black bob has become platinum silver and her usual black cat's eyeglasses now have purple frames. Her black Chanel suit has been accented with multiple strands of chunky, lavender pearls. Other than a slight tweaking of the thick, arched brows, a concession to the fashion of the early millennium, her face remains unchanged by the passing decades in Sin City. Even across from him, her short stature means he's looking down at his companion.

"Thank you. May I have a glass of water and a menu, please?" Michelle always orders in an efficient manner.

"Of course, ma'am."

"I can't tell...is this a drink or a bouquet?" Michelle says after the bartender has left. She picks four edible flowers out of her glass and puts them on Robbie's calamari plate.

"You wanted the trending drink. Caligula's Cosmo is all the rage, or so says the bartender." Robbie bites into one of the discarded flowers. "Tasty."

"You look better than I was led to believe." Michelle picks up Robbie's menu instead of waiting on the waiter. When he shoots her a look, she responds, "You always order the cheeseburger anyway."

"You know what they say: There's no disease that a week in Palm Springs and a good doctor can't fix," he says, hoping to put a casual spin on his problems.

"Who says that? The tourism board of Palm Springs? We both know what disease you have. And I mean addiction, not HIV. I can overlook the overdose for now, but you've got to want to quit." She looks him straight in the eye.

"I'm tapering. Cold turkey is torture. I know I'm getting older. Do you think I want to die sooner than later?" His voice quavers a bit, and he's being more honest than he planned.

"Robbie, baby, you've got to taper off like you mean it. Can you promise me you'll try? Let me give you a business card. I'd like you to see a real doctor for once. First visit's on me. I want someone normal to talk to you."

He wants to defend Doctor Olga, but he can't think of anything to say. Robbie takes the card and knows he doesn't have a choice in the matter.

"Cheer up, Robbie. Let's get you that cheeseburger, and I'll get the Caesar salad." Michelle opens the vast book of an indecipherable menu with Roman numerals. "Let's talk about the show. John Tuckman's getting a lot of fan mail. Why don't you take a week off and really go to Palm Springs? We could have a week of food segments."

"You're not giving MY show to that Australian prick. If I agree to that, it's just for a week," he retorts.

She takes a deep breath. "I want to keep your show going. I watch it every night with Tickles. Even the cat laughs at your jokes. But, if I give Tuckman his own show, think of the cross promotion! I could be the Oprah of Las Vegas. And you get Tuckman out of your hair."

"Where's he going to film? The Silver Rush only has one basement, and it's occupied." He's not budging. He crosses his arms over his chest and sticks out his chin.

"What if you had your own studio in L.A.? A real one? I'm in talks to get you syndicated." She glides her fork over a lettuce leaf as if searching for contaminants.

"I'd say you were putting me on, but I'm listening."

"Think BIG, Robbie. Dreams really do come true. Maybe you've been wandering the desert of local programming for 40 years and you're coming into all the milk and honey in the promised land of syndication."

"I'm the Moses of late night. But the show's only 20 years old." He is a Vegas icon, after all.

"You're getting out of the desert early. But you need to get a handle on those personal demons. You've got to, for the show."

"This is the chance of a lifetime! I know that. I'm not going to screw up."

Michelle leans closer, her pearls dangling over the salad. She grabs Robbie's necktie but doesn't pull. "If you screw up, if the drugs get in the way, I WILL SQUEEZE YOU! Don't test me." She lets go of the tie and relaxes her posture, but her eyes lock with his.

"Yes, ma'am. No drugs, just talk." He puts up his palms as if to surrender.

"And if you ever let your guard down, think I'm not watching you, just know, I am watching you. Right now, I'm using the carrot—not the stick."

"I'll take the carrot." Really, he should have been syndicated ten years ago. Maybe he wouldn't have misspent so much time then. He feels the strange shiver of a gambler about to win a jackpot.

"Good. Let's leave it at that. I'll call you from L.A. in a few days."

"What about my ratings going up...and my discoveries, Finley and Marshmallow? Don't I get some credit for innovation? And I pulled Tuckman into the mix." He's got to get some positivity into a discussion focused on his addictions.

"Finley brought Marshmallow to you. But you saw an opportunity. And I'm giving you credit. You're moving up. But keep Finley on recurring. That bunny can get obnoxious."

"That's just what I tell him." Robbie grins. "What about Tuckman?"

"Tuckman's getting his own show, isn't he? Believe me, that influenced my decision. Food is so hot right now. You must have an angel watching over you, Robbie, or you're the luckiest man in Vegas. Keep your nose clean. And I mean that in the sense of don't put cocaine in it. I'll be in touch." Michelle wipes the corners of her mouth with a cloth napkin then stands up, smoothing her pencil skirt. She takes her purse off the tufted chair and strides out of the restaurant.

Robbie watches her go and realizes she's left him with the tab.

Robbie takes quick steps down to the basement studio of The Silver Rush. He notices how shabby his office has become; have all the substances meant to give him a boost had the opposite effect? He feels as if he hasn't noticed his surroundings in years, and all the furnishings look dated but not tacky. He's only had coffee this morning, but the shock of reality rushing to his head has a somber effect. Even the hardy fiddle fig leaf by his industrial desk needs watering. Why hasn't he noticed these things?

He sits at the desk in the gray swivel chair and decides nothing here goes to the new L.A. studio. He even does a chair-spin like he did in his father's office as a boy. He looks over at the doorway and sees Gouda about to knock.

"I just wanted you to look over some music sheets for Tuesday's episode," Gouda says as he moves his sunglasses on top of his head.

"Hold that thought. Take a seat, my friend. Big news this morning. How do you feel about a new dawn, a different direction? How did the Israelites feel when Moses parted the Red Sea?"

"Invigorated?"

"Yes, that's a great word. Let's go with that." Robbie stands and paces with his hands folded behind his back. "I've had a visit from the Boss. And it's time to move on to the big-time. L.A., Syndication. Milk and honey. Milk and honey make an intoxicating tonic, and we're going to drink it."

Gouda pauses. "I can commute. I don't actually live in Vegas, you know. Or you would know, if you had ever come out to visit."

"Is that an invitation? Okay. I'm there. I've turned over a new leaf. I'm going to have dinner with each of The Stuffed Hams. Even the guy with the tambourine." Robbie sits on the desk for a moment.

"How does Tuckman fit into this scheme? Or Finley?" Gouda asks.

"Tuckman's getting his own big break. A show dedicated to all things culinary. Finley? His status hasn't changed. Recurring. But he's already spending more time in L.A. with that bananas director. Maybe he'll get a mansion in Laurel Canyon if the bullfighter movie goes anywhere. Who's to say?" Robbie doesn't say that the odds of the movie being much better than *Fidelity* are slim to none.

"I've got a request. I want a prime parking space."

"You're really playing hardball. I'll pass it on to Michelle. A good parking spot equals a million bucks in L.A.." Robbie looks up to see Michelle Wise in the hallway.

She knocks on the threshold and doesn't wait for a response to come inside the office. She's dressed head-to-toe in red-and-white polka dots with kitten heels. "I've talked it over with myself: You're getting that parking spot. Now, run along and work on the music, please. Keep up the good work!"

"Thank you, Ms. Wise." Gouda collects his music sheets and makes an exit.

"Hello, Robbie. I see you're making proper preparations for our big move." She stares at the wilting house plant.

"Thanks for noticing me." Robbie waits for his boss to get to the point.

"Robbie, do you remember Jim Garcia?"

"I'll never forget that son of a bitch. He's banned from the show. He knows that. Nobody punches a guest in my green room! Unless it's me."

"I know he's banned from the show, but he's also producing a huge movie. The buzz is that it's funny. I mean, it's got real writers and actors. Not shitty ones. It goes deep into the jungles of the Vietnam War. I thought you might want a little revenge on Garcia."

"I'm listening."

"The director wants you to do a cameo in the movie. You'd be playing a talk show host interviewing the hero. He wants to surprise Garcia, but he also can't think of anyone else for the part."

"Send me the script yesterday," Robbie says. "And negotiate a higher fee. Who's directing?"

"Jeff Savoie."

"Oh my God, that Park Avenue son of a bitch. Yeah, I'll do it."

"I'm glad we're in agreement. One more thing, Robbie. I've taken the liberty of enrolling you in an addiction group-therapy class. They call themselves Resilience Therapy, and the class is about to start in one hour. I've enlisted Gouda to drive you there. I hope you don't mind."

Robbie takes his time to reply to his boss. "I have a feeling it's an offer I can't refuse."

"Something like that. Don't worry, Gouda is hanging around, waiting for you in the parking lot. Goodbye for now. I'm going to work on finding appropriate...*support* for you in Los Angeles as well. I'm just protecting my investment. Don't disappoint me."

"Yes, ma'am." Robbie turns off the lights and walks out to find Gouda waiting for him on the ground floor. He didn't know he had plans tonight.

Robbie finds himself in the basement of a Unitarian church. He sits in a metal folding chair, not a padded one either, in a room decorated only by potted succulents and a beige geometric tapestry. A dozen folding chairs sit in a circle over a faded green area rug. Some of the group members look shabby, and others look healthy. Their ages range from a woman in her early twenties to a man in his seventies. Robbie realizes he's stopped listening and tunes back into the conversation.

"Why couldn't I be there to hold him? Did he know I loved him? Why did he have to die? I wanted to hold him in that moment, but he died alone." A woman with a Midwestern accent says this with tears in her eyes. Even her brown bob quivers as she shakes her head. "I just can't talk about this anymore. I don't want to monopolize the group or anything. I just loved that dog. So much." Her voice quavers.

Robbie wants to say that she's being a bit dramatic. She's talking about her family dog that died of old age. But he remains silent out of tact. He looks over at Gouda and realizes that everyone in the group has spoken except him. He has to participate in this, or he'll hear about it from Michelle. He raises a hand, and the therapist nods at him to proceed.

"My name is Robbie Roberts and I'm a drug addict."

The therapist holds out a French-manicured hand to stop him. She crosses her legs and shuffles the papers on her lap. "Mr. Roberts, this is not an AA meeting. You don't have to be so formal. But please continue. We welcome your input."

"I love the pleasure of drugs. I love heroin; I love speedballs, but those are treats, candy, occasional. It's like a fucking orgasm in your brain. But it's deadly. It will ruin my face. It will ruin my TV career. So, I just take a hit of cocaine. It's like morning coffee. I take it after coffee. Cocaine just helps me function. What's wrong with that? I mean, I know it's wrong, but I love it. That's why I'm here."

"What if I told you that cocaine doesn't help you function? That you don't need it? That you're lying to yourself." The therapist leans forward and makes eye contact.

"Right now, I can't imagine life without coke. I can promise to taper off, but that's where I am. Breakfast coke."

"I appreciate the honesty here. But I want you to be honest with yourself. Give us an example of a time cocaine was destructive in your life. I think it would be good for the group to hear the whole story."

"I did this interview about ten years ago. I took a little extra cocaine that morning. I was on edge. I was interviewing Kevin Luker with his bunny puppet, Marshmallow. I didn't want the interview to be kid stuff, so I kept needling him. I didn't let up. I started talking shit about the bunny and the show. Like saying she was fucking Sugar Sam, her co-star. He got tense, and nobody liked the interview. It didn't land. When he died of pneumonia a few weeks later, I felt fucking horrible about the whole thing." Robbie exhales and runs a hand over his salt-and-pepper hair.

"So, there were consequences." She leans back a little.

"Let me interject here," a middle-aged man with glasses says. "My daughter watched that show. She loved that bunny. What you did was disgusting. Repulsive. I don't really think you made up for it. You're a piece of work."

The therapist holds up a hand. "Roger, we're here to help Robbie. He can't change the past, but he can change his future."

"I am helping him. I want him to know that his past stinks." Roger crosses his arms over his sweater vest.

"Alright, you've voiced your opinion. Let's give Robbie the floor back now."

"Yeah, he's right, but I tried to fix it. I hired his son and helped him get started in the industry. I mean, he found me, so I guess he fixed it. But it gave me...closure."

The therapist begins to applaud, and the rest of the group joins in. Even Roger claps a few times. Gouda looks a bit relieved that Robbie may be making progress. "We've heard from everyone in the group except for you." She turns to Gouda.

"I'm here to support this guy. My name is Choi, but he calls me by my stage name, Gouda, which is a delicious smoked cheese." He points at Robbie in the folding chair beside him. "Robbie has problems with narcotics and opioids, but I have problems with alcohol. I like to drink when I'm writing music, but it doesn't really make the music any better. It's just me...lying to myself. I gave up smoking though. If you're a trumpeter, it can really mess with your breath control. I think I'm moving forward in a good direction."

"That's wonderful, Choi. We don't exactly have sponsors here, but there's nothing wrong with being a supportive friend."

Roger raises his hand. "I want to add a few things to my mental health check-in. If you don't mind."

The therapist looks at the clock. "We have a few minutes before we end with guided therapy. Please be brief."

"I've been coming back to my addiction a few times this month. I'm depressed that my singing career isn't panning out. I can't even do open mic nights because my guitarist is out of town. So, I keep eating paste. Sometimes I tear up a sheet of paper and mix it in the paste. I can't seem to stop. But I'm going to taper off like Robbie suggested." Roger looks hopeful at the prospect.

Robbie covers his face to keep from laughing at Roger's earnest declaration about eating paste.

"I'm glad this session has been helpful for you. Let's dive into the last portion of our group meeting. Guided meditation. You may sit or lie comfortably. You can close your eyes or leave them open. Imagine a place, a happy place. Maybe it's the college quad where you fell in love for the first time. Imagine the wind blowing tree branches around a quiet wooded scene. Maybe you're sitting in the grass. Look around you. You feel at peace. Wiggle your toes. Now, let's focus on our breathing. Take a deep breath through your nose. Now, slowly exhale. Imagine you're breathing in strength and exhaling your addiction. Breath in good, fresh air, exhale your addiction. You're at peace in the sunshine. The breeze blows through your hair. Breathe in the sunshine, breathe out your addiction. Let it go. Now, let your mind wander to wherever it wants to go. Now, let that go. Open your eyes on the last beautiful breath. Exhale all negativity. Love yourself. Let's give ourselves a big hand!"

Robbie claps along with the group, but he doesn't feel much. Back when he started the show, the set became his happy place. He realizes that maybe he'd been happier before his addiction had progressed to something he couldn't handle on his own. Maybe he would come back to the Resilience Group and give the New Age bullshit another chance. Maybe he could even remember the therapist's name next time; it was something dull as rocks.

In the aftermath of the bachelor party, the premiere of *Fidelity,* and finding himself the odd man out in Andrea's sea of troubled wedding plans, Finley gladly volunteers to man the Sparkle, Inc. booth at a small comic expo in Arizona. Mr. Sparkle is away on a mysterious trip and Scott has retreated to his bedroom, so no one else was available.

He arrives at a faded Phoenix hotel ballroom with boxes of *Mr. Glitz* comics dating back to the '70s. Sensing his friend Robbie's mental state after the last talk show filming, he asked him to come along. Robbie had been reading up on the orangutan's dubious attempts to glamorize his corner of jungle habitat throughout the long road trip.

"The art's not bad," he says in a grudging way. "I'll catch up later. Need some coffee." Robbie puts on his sunglasses and disappears, headed for the hotel's restaurant.

The harried organizer instructs Finley to take a table at the end of a row. A plump man in shorts, he sports a luxurious beard and longish hair.

"What do I tell the taco truck?" A woman interrupts.

"Tell them they need more *pico de gallo,*" the bearded man teases.

"Avery!"

"I'll talk to them in a minute!" He continues walking with Finley.

"There's still a Mr. Glitz cult in the Southwest. Mostly gay men nostalgic for what it brought to their childhoods— some women, too. You'll sell some copies. It sold pretty well in its day. Mr. Sparkle should consider one more comic for the fans."

"I'll tell him that, thanks." Finley looks around at the vendors: a kaleidoscope of lesser-known pop culture memorabilia. Finley does his best to display the comics and various plush orangutans, but he feels particular pride at placing Marshmallow right next to Mr. Glitz. He's even brought a stack of the single Marshmallow comic series released in the 1990s to tie in with the show. Waiting for the expo to officially open, he leafs through the story of Sugar Sam's journey to Sugarcane Valley to find Marshmallow's secret treasure chest of marshmallows.

After an hour alone at the table, Finley wants to stretch his legs. He sees Robbie walking towards him with a cheese Danish and coffee in a Styrofoam cup.

"A peace offering. Sorry I took off," Robbie says with a mouthful of cheese Danish.

"Uh, thanks. Do you mind taking over? I want to see the stuff here." Finley motions towards the shabby displays of forgotten pop culture scattered before him. He takes a large bite out of the Danish.

Robbie suddenly realizes that his knowledge of the Mr. Glitz series has limitations. "I don't know about this stuff. I'm in no hurry to see it, so I guess I'm taking over this operation. What do I say anyway? Is there an official Sparkle, Incorporated sales pitch?"

"Just wing it like you do your show."

"Asshole!"

"See you in a few days," Finley jokes. He'll probably be back in a few minutes because there isn't much to see.

"Asshole!" Robbie starts straightening up the table and takes off his sunglasses.

Finley notices a booth with a comic series called *Planet of the Ro-mans*. The Ro-mans look sort of like someone put a diving helmet on top of a gorilla suit. He flips through a comic, and the woman at the table notices him.

"What do you think of it?" she says and stares at him.

What does he think of it? Alien robot gorillas on a dying planet? Why do they need diving helmets; do they ever dive? They always seem to be flailing about in rage and threatening nuclear holocausts, even in the few pages he can see. Ro-man reports to an identical Ro-man about getting cold feet regarding the destruction of Earth. *"I must! But I cannot!"* Ro-man screams on multiple pages.

"Certainly unique. The art has a dream-like quality." Finley pauses on a page with a Ro-man picking up a beautiful woman and carrying her into a cave. "Which issue should I pick?"

"Issue 9. You'll never forget it." She smiles in a mysterious way, eyes cloudy through thick glasses under a mustard-colored beret.

"What inspires you?" Finley looks up, eyebrows knitting together.

"The story behind the film *Robot Monster*. You see, the director thought he was making *Citizen Kane* or something. He had a friend with a gorilla suit, and he stuck a diving helmet on top. He had lines and lines written about nuclear war; he thought it was the best movie ever made. But everyone else just saw it as a bad drive-in Grade Z movie. The director had a breakdown. They put him in an asylum after he read the bad reviews. But he recovered and became a camera guy on '80s shows or something. To me, it's a metaphor for creativity," she says in one breath, as if a practiced monologue.

Finley nods. He understands creativity in the way only an actor who knows his movie has been doomed from the beginning could know. She reminds him of Provocateur a little. Passion really may be the most important quality in any kind of creative personality, he reasons. "Maybe that's all we can hope for in any work of art: getting towards the metaphor." Finley smiles at her. He pays for a few issues of the comic and walks over to the next display. He looks at her one last time to see her doodling another man in a gorilla suit and diving helmet.

Finley stares at a tall yeti plush standing over the comics in the next vendor booth. Its long eyelashes seem feminine. *Snow Lovers* has multiple issues. He thumbs through the first comic. A French explorer becomes stranded in a snowy cave in Tibet, not knowing it is a yeti cave. The yeti nurses him back to health, and the two "snow-lovers" slowly become more than friends. Finley has to stifle a laugh at the first furry white embrace.

The author clears his throat. He responds, "This isn't a library, you know!" The pale man looks indignant.

"I'm sorry. I'll take the first two comics." He looks at the titles, "Snowbound" and "Not Yeti" and feels morbid curiosity. It might be fun to leave these on the coffee table of the *Robbie Roberts Tonight!* set.

"Here's my card. You might want to finish the series."

Finley feels a wave of disgust about accepting the card, but he struggles to smile at the vendor. He's read enough for now. He notices the name on the card, **Snow E. Cave**, and the smile becomes real.

MR. SPARKLE'S

TWILIGHT

Chas Sparkle delights in his daughter's upcoming nuptials. He pauses for lunch after running errands. He steps from his home and stands at the Laga Brutto Fountains. The tasks are mostly related to the fitting of the Versace gown and ensuring the luxe wedding cake dazzles the guests. On mild desert mornings, the scent of flowers lazily drifts towards the nose without the tobacco smoke that hung over the city in decades past. Lately, the scent of marijuana bullies its way into the mix but, today, he can smell the flowers curious to the West.

Speaking of flowers, Andrea settled on a golden swan theme for the event, but finding a florist to create an enormous floral installation depicting a giant swan has been daunting—even in Vegas. At least, reflects Chas, such an aesthetic monstrosity will delight the noses of wedding guests. The swan seems an appropriate symbol even though the groom is more of a goose who's just laid an egg by appearing as Fidel Castro. Mr. Sparkle can only hope that a Razzie nomination will be forthcoming. In the year of Halle Berry's fur ball of a movie, *Cat Woman*, he fears the Razzies might pass over Finley's mediocre film, but there's always hope. Maybe the new movie will be better.

After fun wedding errands, Chas knows he faces an unpleasant task: getting his ex-wife ready for the wedding. Andrea believes her mother is back in Long Beach. Andrea never knew about the heroin and doesn't know Nancy has been in rehab near Las Vegas. Chas tracked her down in New York when he heard about Andrea and Finley's engagement, hoping to get her clean and presentable for the wedding. He'd even bribed her with a designer mother-of-the-bride dress, although *he'll* probably steal the show with pearl embroidery on a dove-gray tuxedo.

After stopping to buy Lorraine's favorite Asiatic lilies, Chas waits in the green waiting room at The Ledges Rehabilitation Center. The quiet unsettles him more than the ticking of a hideous bronze clock. A hatchet-faced woman lights a cigarette, disregarding him and every **no smoking** sign in the building. He stares at her painted eyebrows and moves the seats a bit closer to the window. Lorraine is now 20 minutes late. How could she do this to him, leaving him in an antiseptic nightmare of a waiting room? He picks up *Vanity Fair* and wonders if Courteney Cox has had something done to her face. Should he get another nip and tuck?

Finally, a thinner woman comes out to meet him, her mascara smudged from tears, as usual.

He kisses her cheek and says his catchphrase for her. "Lovely, like a lily!"

She does smile as he gives her the flowers. "How are you these days? Yous getting enough to eat?" She speaks in a childish Long Island sing-song whisper.

"Right as rainbows! But how are you, darling? Are you ready for a wedding?" He holds her limp hand reassuringly.

"We got to go to Francine's for the trousseau. She'll need satin slippers: she's tall. Something borrowed. Gotta get Desiree to gimme Grandma Maria's veil. She owes me that," she says flatly, staring at nothing in front of her.

He stares for a moment. She'd voiced this outrageous request to fly to Long Island, NY, on his dime as if it is already reality. The flight will be booked; Scott must be left home, of course. She'll insist on staying with her sister while he'll have to stay elsewhere—far away from the snoring of both women.

She knows he'll do all of this for Andrea's perfect day.

"We can have coffee at the Bayside Diner. We can have ice cream?" She finally focuses her eyes on him.

"Yes, we can have ice cream. Mister Softee or Carvel."

"Let's not go crazy now! Can you sing to me before we go? 'Chasaroonie,' please."

Chas doesn't mind singing a bit, especially if it bothers the impersonal staff or the obnoxious lady with the cigarette.

He's seen his fair share of tough crowds. He wonders if he can perform with Scott for charity at rehabs all over Las Vegas, but he puts the thought on the back-burner. He warms up with a vocal exercise. Although he doesn't have the voice of a crooner, he can still try for Lorraine. *"Move your feet and start to tap! Don't you worry 'bout a misstep. Keep on moving your view to the happy avenue!"*

Surprisingly, the woman with the cigarette starts to smile and looks less frightening. She starts tapping her toes.

He tries to get Lorraine to move, so they can walk out the door to the last line: *"To that happy avenue!"*

He hears her harmonizing, the voice unsteady and sometimes offkey, but it's great to hear her singing again.

He's got to check her in for the night; he's even paying a Sparkle, Inc. intern to babysit her in a suite. He brings Lorraine's luggage, a small bag of old clothes, into a generous Laga Brutto suite. The intern talks on the phone while Lorraine watches a game show rerun with glazed eyes. There's no question of him bringing her back to his house with Scott there. Chas dreads packing and hearing his husband's protests all over again.

He turns the key and enters a silent home. He can already feel Scott seething. Scott is finishing coffee in the dining room and, if looks could kill, Chas might be concerned about his well-being.

"Well, the prodigal husband returns from a visit with Satan. And don't say she's the mother of your child," Scott comes out swinging.

"She wants to go to Long Island...for the trousseau. She wants a perfect mother-of-the-bride dress," Chas replies in a whisper.

"Oh, my God. Oh, my God! The nerve of that bitch! And you're going? At least you didn't bring her here. To the scene of attempted MURDER. 29 stitches. 29 stitches, Chas! Do you know I'm a saint for staying with you?" Scott pauses and looks at Chas.

Chas says nothing.

"And saying goodbye to all the money you give to the endless cause of keeping that heroin addict alive?!" Scott has tears in his eyes, and Chas can't stand it. Scott pounds the dining table with a balled fist, and coffee spills onto the ivory French linen. Both men ignore the stain.

"I'll make it up to you. We'll go to Fiji. I'll take that pottery class you want. Just get through the wedding. For Andrea," he pleads while stroking Scott's arm. "Please."

"You know, she's a fake. Mother of the bride, my ass. We're the only parents Andrea has."

Chas bristles at the more obtrusive security at JFK and prays that Lorraine hasn't snuck any drug paraphernalia into the suitcase he'd given her. He'd been relieved they made it through security in Vegas, but one never knows with his ex-wife; she might have met a dealer on the flight. She'd picked out a ghastly hot-pink, giraffe-print carry-on, and he sees her still clinging to it like a security blanket. Her damp hair sticks to her temples, and she takes slow steps in velour slippers, the unofficial footwear of rehabilitation.

He takes longer strides to get to the baggage claim; Chas is accustomed to a fast pace like all native New Yorkers. He turns and sees Lorraine has dropped her bag in the middle of the airport and is bending down to pick it up. She continues her dazed walk towards baggage claim, but he knows she's seen him and turns his attention at looking for her giraffe-print suitcase and his faux-crocodile bag. His Long Island cousin, Joseph Rizzo, is lending him a condominium on Long Beach; at least there'll be no fuss with checking into a hotel.

"Are we taking a shuttle?" Lorraine whispers. "I can't take the motion anymore. I'll throw up." Tears form in her eyes.

Chas grabs the two bags off the conveyer belt and moves her out of the way of a family.

A Japanese man nods as they pass.

"Cousin Joey is picking us up. We can eat out if you want to. He made reservations in Long Beach. But we could spend a day in the City." He wouldn't mind seeing the Empire State Building again.

"Oh, really? That's nice. I don't want to go to the City. I don't want to see where the Towers used to be; it's so sad, you know? They didn't even let me watch the news when it happened." She puts her head down and shuffles along.

Chas continues walking out of the terminal. He doesn't want to discuss the World Trade Center with Lorraine of all people. He just wants to get through this trip. "It was a tragedy," he says.

"Does Joey still have the Chrysler? The talking car that says, 'The door is ajar' like a robot?" Her voice brightens.

"No, he sold that it in the '80s. He told me to look for a black Jaguar." He scans the parking lot, but the plane landed right on schedule so Joey may not be there.

They step outside, and Lorraine looks around her. "We're back in NY, Chas! I think we're going to have fun." She twirls in the cool air as if a model in her twenties.

Chas thinks of Scott and remembers that his spouse is having anything but fun. He'll have to deal with the aftermath of this trip. Scott will never see Lorraine as anything but evil.

Chas sees a black Jaguar pull up and notices a giant Mr. Glitz plush in the backseat. It's Joey alright, just a bit heavier and with a head full of silver hair.

"Chas! Long time no see. Nice to see you, Lorraine." Joey kisses her on the cheek then puts their bags in the trunk. They all buckle up with Chas riding shotgun and Lorraine in the backseat with Mr. Glitz. Joey turns up the volume of a KISS song and exits the airport. "Everyone's excited about the wedding. Is this Finley a decent guy? Is he treating her right?" Joey zigs and zags through the traffic and merges on the Long Island Expressway.

"She likes him. Scott talks to him more than I do, but it could work out," Chas reflects on his houseguest and smiles.

"I think he's handsome," Lorraine adds.

"What kind of work does he do?" Joey asks while nearly running a red light. "Hey, get out of the way, asshole!"

he shouts after a Honda Civic, tapping the exterior of the Jaguar with an open hand.

The response from the other driver remains inaudible, but the tone sends all the message needed.

Joey ignores this and changes lanes again.

"He's an actor. He was in that movie *Fidelity*," Chas says while holding his seatbelt as Joey makes a sharp turn.

"Didn't see it. What's it about?" Joey merges into the HOV lane, speeding.

"Umm... He plays Fidel Castro," Chas says.

"No shit. Commie bullshit movie. Don't be offended if I don't watch." Joey nods as if he's made up his mind. "Okay, I'll talk to this guy at the wedding and knock some American sense into his head."

"That's fine with me. But he's so good-looking," Lorraine says.

"He's going to film a movie in Spain for the same director," Chas points out. "This new movie has nothing to do with Fidel Castro."

"What's the director's name?" Joey continues moving at ever-terrifying velocities.

"Provocateur. He won an award at the Cannes Film Festival." Chas grips the seat.

"Jesus. French stuff. Finley's case gets worse and worse." Joey turns, and Chas feels relief that they must be nearing the condominium.

Chas begins his day bright and early at ten o'clock, early for Lorraine anyway. Maybe most of her troubles begin with the antisocial tendency of being a night person, he theorizes. Night people either tend to get into show business or into trouble. They walk to the bagel shop, Lorraine shutting out the sun with a hat. A scarf wraps around the hat, and sunglasses sit on the brim. Chas wishes she'd walk faster, but he tries to be patient.

"Order me an everything bagel with cream cheese and lox," she instructs then pivots to sit at a café table by the window. The morning crowd has dissipated, but some bagels remain for late morning customers.

After he gets their order, he watches her deconstruct her bagel as she always does, eating the lox first then cutting up the quartered bagel into eighths on wax paper.

"Don't forget we've got an appointment at Francine's at one. We've got to catch our train to get there." He's already finished his buttered raisin bagel and sips on black coffee.

"Yeah, yeah. I'm eating as fast as I can. Now, what did you say is the color scheme for the wedding? I'd never wear white like your mother did at our wedding." Lorraine won't forgive Mrs. Rizzo after 30 years.

"It was eggshell," Chas defends his mother.

"I really want a lilac dress. Organza? I need a necklace and shoes dyed to match, of course. Do you think we could get into Tiffany's? Jewelry would make me so beautiful." She nibbles along the edges of her bagel.

"Purple, white, and gold are the colors she picked. I think the dress will show itself to you there. You just have to say, 'Yes.' I'm not sure about organza, but the color sounds right."

"You're going to be there when I come out of the fitting room, aren't you? I need an opinion." She pouts as if he's planning to leave her at Francine's.

"I'll sit right outside the fitting room. But I don't think we're going to Tiffany's. Francine's has plenty of accessories made to match. You might find a necklace there," Chas deflects. He can't imagine Scott's fury if he bought Lorraine jewelry from Tiffany's.

"I'm done with this bagel. They never butter the middle enough, but the lox was fine." She's made a pile of bagel pieces on her plate like a Picasso arrangement. "Would you mind throwing it away?" She closes her eyes as if to make the trash disappear.

They find themselves aboard the Long Island Rail Road, and Chas watches the scenery unfold through the window. The fall foliage adds color and beauty, but he almost misses the lively graffiti on the trains of the '70s. The whole place seems sanitized and more serene than the urban jungle of Las Vegas.

He looks over at Lorraine and hears a snore. She sleeps more without the stimulants she'd taken in the past. He doesn't want to wake her up, but they can't miss the appointment. She resembles Andrea when her face relaxes but with a reddish complexion and straight, fine hair, while Andrea's hair is dark and thick. Lorraine may not have taken care of her skin or health, but the good bones still show themselves in her face.

He remembers when he'd helped Lorraine pick out her wedding dress from Francine's once he realized her mother had hideous fashion sense. Their wedding photos look classic, although he doesn't display them anywhere Scott would see.

The multi-story fashion temple goes on for days, and they take an escalator up to the third floor. He notices a man he recognizes behind a station, wearing a familiar bow tie and vest but with a face 30 years older. Or maybe it's a coincidence.

The brisk personal shopper named Luann picks several dresses in purple hues for Lorraine to try. Luann even draws Lorraine's name in calligraphy on a fitting room door.   Chas takes a seat on a white velvet chair and waits for the first dress.

The organza doesn't suit Lorraine, and the effect is something like Bette Davis's frightening dress from *What Ever Happened to Baby Jane?* so Chas has to withhold his scathing comments.

"The color is flattering but I don't like the skirt. It's too flouncy. I think you'd look great in something more structured." He doesn't add "more age-appropriate."

She swishes the skirt in the mirror. "I want to dance. This dress makes me want to dance. But I'll try on the others." She heads back to the fitting room.

The next gown stuns him. Its beaded illusion neckline glides into deep-purple jersey fabric that flatteringly skims the body and features a daring side-slit. She looks at herself in several mirrors, and even she must admit this dress succeeds in ways that her first pick did not.

"I remember Gladys, the old sales lady here. She told me that, 'Just because it looks good on the hanger, doesn't mean it looks good on you.' I didn't like this dress on the hanger, but the personal shopper told me to try it on. It doesn't swish, though! I get to dance with Finley, and I want to *swish* and *swish.*" She looks at her elegant reflection as if doubting the dress's ability.

Chas clears his throat and struggles to remain tactful. "I love this dress, but you've got others to try on." He'll have to see the rest before he puts up a fight for his favorite.

Lorraine heads back to the dressing room, and Chas notices the attendant rushing over with new gowns.

He's surprised she's not tripping in her stiletto heels and long skirt, but she must have practiced quite a bit. He thumbs through the Francine's winter catalog and notes that strapless styles are making a comeback and wishes overly plucked eyebrows were out of fashion.

After an interminable amount of time, Lorraine walks to the mirror as if on a catwalk during Fashion Week. The lavender dress has a mermaid cut and another daring slit, but this gown catches the light with beading and sequins.

Chas prefers the second dress's neckline and darker shade of purple but sees from Lorraine's glowing smile that she has found the dress.

"I'll shine like a star at the wedding! Not as brightly as Andrea, but I'm mother of the bride! But that doesn't mean I have to look like a mother of the bride." She twists and turns in the mirror.

Chas walks over to check out the price tag. The gown has not gone on sale, and it will cost him $2,000. He imagines Scott confronting him with the credit card bill in hand months from now, but ending this little shopping trip early will be worth the consequence. "We'll go with this one then."

"Luann is wrapping the beautiful gown up for me. They'll even ship it back to Vegas. I gave her your address. Now, I need purple heels. Very high. I can get away with it, I'm petite." She touches every dress on a rack that catches her eye as if it's a ritual and she's losing focus.

Chas wants to point out that her height of 5'6" rises above the definition of petite, but he remembers tact. He grips a rack to steady himself as she flips through dress after dress. He remembers shopping with Lorraine in their high school days, and Lorraine would fixate on the evening gowns and mink coats for hours. They'd even skip school to go to Macy's. He remembers his grievance of the white mink he'd given her after Andrea's birth. The one she'd pawned to get drugs. Too many memories flood him, and he feels dizzy.

"I noticed a gemstone necklace that would match the gown on the second floor," he says to distract her.

"Yes. The second floor. Shoes on the first."

They take the stairs rather than the elevator because Chas likes to get in exercise at his age.

Lorraine stops halfway down the elegant staircase and begins coughing. The crystal chandelier seems to vibrate with the force of her cough. One cough cascades into a paroxysm and she has to sit down on a step. He wonders if they should visit a doctor, but the coughs end. Lorraine has always had a snore that reverberates with more force than a jet engine, but she refuses to have it checked out by a doctor. She has always had a cough, but this coughing fit seems unusual.

"Do you need to go back to the condominium? We can come back here tomorrow."

"Let's just get some hot tea across the street and come back. Please?"

He nods and helps her down the staircase. "Are you okay? Maybe we should see a doctor. Do they give you physical in rehab?"

She shakes her head. "Not really. They waltz in your room and turn on all the lights on at 4:30 in the morning," she whispers, not wanting to be overheard. "They take your blood pressure, and then they leave. It's horrible. It's worse than group therapy. One of my roommates would scream and curse at them, and there wasn't anything I could do about it. Stupid white coats."

"Why don't you order some hot tea while I pay for the gown?" he asks, pressing a twenty-dollar bill into her clammy hand. He helps her stand, and she hangs onto the handrail all the way down. He leaves her to go to the first floor to pay Luann for the gown and accessories that will arrive in Vegas in time.

Chas walks outside, into a humid haze of an autumn afternoon. He doesn't notice anything amiss until he nears the coffee shop and sees Lorraine passed out on the sidewalk. He considers calling Joey but calls 911 instead. He checks for a pulse and doesn't move her but stays near on the sidewalk.

The EMTs show up after a lifetime.

Lorraine still hasn't regained consciousness.

"Will she be alright?" he asks after they load her into the ambulance.

"Hard to say. I don't think it's a heart attack, but I'm not sure what's going on. You'll have to wait for the doctor. You can call the hospital to find out what room she's in."

Chas takes the Long Island train back to Long Beach.

"Where's Lorraine?" Joey looks up from the episode of *Seinfeld*.

"She passed out on the sidewalk."

"Jesus. Is it heroin?" Joey stares at him for a second.

"I haven't seen her using."

"Come on, Chas. She's a heroin addict. New York City's like a candy store. It's a shopping carnival for addicts."

"We don't know that yet. I haven't seen her using. Lorraine really wants to stay clean for Andrea."

"Like she even cares about Andrea. I can't believe she remembers she has a daughter."

"I hear this from Scott. I don't need to hear it from you."

"Scott's a wise man. Maybe you should listen."

"Lorraine is the mother of my child. And she was my friend a long time ago. And my wife. She may not have much longer to live."

"All of us are dying! Cry me a river. I didn't do heroin, though."

"You sure can smoke. And those Pringles aren't prolonging your life."

You got me. Okay, I'm being asshole. Do you need me to drive you to the hospital?"

"Yeah."

Chas and Joey walk into the hospital, searching for the mysterious Room 1127. The door stands halfway open, a shocking shade of brown beside hundreds of feet of ecru brick wall. Chas notices a wizened figure near death in an oxygen tent, but he realizes she must be the roommate and sees a serene, unconscious Lorraine in the next bed.

"Dehydration," a raspy, matter-of-fact voice says.

The bent figure of a woman in the depths of middle age and osteoporosis sits in the only chair. Chas recognizes her as Lorraine's sister, Desiree, but his mind takes several moments to remember. He has not seen her since Scott banished her from their home for stealing candle sticks and untold numbers of gimcrackery from the piano room.

He embraces the fragile woman. Maintaining a slim physique without adequate nutrition during her years as a ballerina took a terrible toll. Despite Lorraine's decades of body abuse through heroin, it's difficult to surmise that Desiree is the younger sister. Desiree has zipped herself into an ice-blue evening gown, perhaps a Halston original design, well-preserved but purchased during her heyday in the '70s. Chas remembers telling her and Lorraine to "look like a star!" in younger days, but who wears an evening gown to a hospital visit?

Desiree stands up to shake his hand. "I haven't RSVP'd to the wedding, but I'd like to go with Joey and Lorraine. I'm excited for our beautiful Andrea!" Desiree says as if she's received an invitation.

"Of course. We're looking forward to it." Chas wonders which hotel he can book to keep her far away from his house. Although he has some sympathy for Desiree's constant struggle to keep up the appearance of wealth and class, he doesn't want to be the victim of her kleptomania ever again.

"Don't worry about Lorraine. Her baby sister is here now. Why don't you go have something to eat?" She grasps Lorraine's hand through the hospital sheet. She makes a show of fluffing the pillow and smoothing the blanket.

Joey grabs a Jell-O from Lorraine's untouched tray and sits down to eat it. "Has she woken up? What did the doctor say? When can she go home? Chas has to get back to Vegas. He can't stay at my place forever."

"He said that she has to stay overnight, at least to let the IV do its job. He thinks she had pneumonia. That rehab wasn't taking care of her. I don't think she should fly back to

Vegas any time soon. I can look after her. She's my sister. I'll get her to the wedding." Desiree nods as she makes the decision.

"She was acting funny at the airport. But I really haven't spent enough time with her lately to know that she wasn't well. I'm so sorry about this. I can stay for a little while longer, and I'll keep visiting. Her gown is being sent back to Vegas, and she's going to look beautiful for the wedding. I'll even make her a hair appointment." Chas tries to brighten the mood in the arid room.

"I could use a hair appointment." Desiree touches her own short hair.

"Of course, darling. Anything for Andrea's Aunt Desiree." Chas pats her shoulder.

"I don't understand," Joey says from the ugly yellow recliner.

"Understand what?" Desiree asks in disbelief.

"How do people get dehydrated? It's never happened to me. I mean, everybody has tap water. Why wouldn't you drink if you were thirsty?" He scoops a clump of lime Jell-O into his mouth after he ponders his own question.

"I don't know. That's why we have medical doctors. That's all we need to know until Lorraine wakes up." Desiree has no interest in the origins of dehydration.

"You rang?" a voice asks from the doorway. "Medical doctor here. How's our patient?" A woman in her thirties looks at Lorraine and checks the IV. "I'd like to speak with a relative if I may."

"That would be Desiree. I'm only an ex-husband, I'm afraid. And Joey's just an ex-husband's cousin." Chas motions to Joey to get out of the chair.

His cousin grabs an orange juice off the tray, and they head out the long corridor towards the elevator.

Chas stares at the buttons on the way down and feels a pang of guilt. He remembers skipping school with Lorraine when they went to Roosevelt just to window-shop at Bloomingdale's. Maybe they'd never really been married in the traditional way, but she had been his friend.

Maybe they could still be friends.

Back in Las Vegas, Chas has arranged a compromise to unruffle Scott's feathers: Lorraine will not be present at the historic choosing of the bride's dress. Only Scott and Chas will assist Andrea in the selection at Versace.

Andrea wants to be daring, beautiful, and traditional all at once, and Scott feels she should consider the simplicity of Vera Wang, but Andrea will not budge on the point. She must wear a Versace creation on her special day.

The Versace attendant, Victoria, offers minimalistic service, and Andrea can't decide which silhouette she'd like on the dress. She ponders a shorter reception gown to show off her legs, one of her best assets, but a ballgown would show off her slim waist.

Chas and Scott sit on a sofa in front of a myriad of mirrors and fresh flowers. Scott has said little this morning, only nibbling the edges of a cheese Danish and taking his coffee black. He did, however, accept a hug from Chas before they left for the Versace boutique.

Andrea walks out in a mermaid gown with an illusion neckline over lace. She glides like a vision in white, but *is this the dress?*

She stares at her reflection.

The blond attendant smooths the train. "This is truly stunning."

Andrea continues looking at the dress. "Could we possibly alter it? I want to get rid of the illusion neckline. I think it would work if it were strapless."

"That will be no problem, but there will be an added fee."

Andrea nods into the mirror. "Definitely strapless."

Get Me to the Church on Time

Wedding planning is going smoothly. Andrea insists on having the ceremony at the Elvis Chapel on the Strip and the reception at The Laga Brutto; she wants the famous lake of fountains in nearly every photo. She wants her wedding to reflect Las Vegas in every possible way.

Finley turns to his luminous fiancée as they hold hands on a stroll to a fancy bakery for the corny traditional cake-tasting. "I've been meaning to ask about the guest list. Are we inviting your mother?"

Andrea's face takes on a pallor. "I haven't told you much. Did you read tabloids in the '80s?"

"No." Finley gets a sinking feeling.

"She knew Dad was gay but, back then, it helped an entertainer to have a beard. Certainly, when he started the *Mr. Glitz* comic strip in the *Las Vegas Review-Journal*, he had to lay low. I mean, Shultz was a Sunday school teacher when he was doing *Peanuts*, you know? It kind of stinks that no one had a problem with Schultz or Dr. Seuss or your dad cheating on their wives but, goddamn, my dad wasn't allowed to be gay." She looks at the grass growing near the bakery for a minute then resumes, "Mom told him she just didn't want him bringing men to their house. But, one day, she caught him in the bedroom with Scott. I was at my grandmother's house, thank God. I was about seven. She got the butcher knife and went after Scott. Dad had to call the police. She gave Dad full custody as long as he dropped the charges. She moved back to

Long Beach, and I haven't seen her in about ten years. But, yes, I want Mom there. Every girl does, doesn't she?"

He squeezes her hand and kisses her. "I'm so sorry that happened to your family. No wonder Scott doesn't want to be anywhere near your mother. I don't blame the guy."

"What about YOUR mother, Finley? And your stepmother?" Andrea breaks the embrace and looks at her fiancé with a soft expression, demure in a sleeveless emerald dress he's never seen before.

"Oh, Mother won't be able to make it. She can't travel anymore. She's able to move about her assisted-living room a bit, but she's mostly in bed. Maybe we can visit her after we come back from Spain."

Andrea nods, knowing about his mother's fragile health.

Finley thinks for a moment about his stepmother. "As for Jennifer? I can't believe it, but she's RSVP'd a **yes**. She penciled in that Chi Chi would be her plus one."

"What in hell is a Chi Chi?" Andrea scrunches her brow.

Finley can't help but laugh. "Chi Chi resembles the kind of hound you might find in Hell. She is the most hideous Chihuahua I've ever seen. She has an underbite."

"Jesus Christ. She's not bringing it to the wedding. Can you make that very clear?"

"What about John Tuckman? Is he still invited? Robbie needs all the support he can get as best man."

"I guess... Just don't seat him too close to me."

The officiant is stuck in traffic. None of his three groomsmen, Robbie, Provocateur, and his high school friend, Jeremy Berry, will arrive until the rehearsal dinner.

Finley doesn't notice his stepmother on first sight, but he recognizes Chi Chi. Breathe, just breathe, Finley tells himself. Jennifer had an extensive facelift to obscure her age, but it renders her unrecognizable. And she's brought a dog into the church! She holds the goddamn Chihuahua in her lap. Jennifer never cared that Finley was allergic to dogs, or so he's told her. Finley can't help but overhear everything Jennifer is whining about to the poor man who let them in Elvis Chapel.

"Well, his father died and his poor mother's in that home after the car accident. My late husband's estate is still paying for her care. God knows for how long? And I've been so generous. I'm paying for the rehearsal dinner, aren't I? And he didn't even recognize me! I'm just glad he's getting married and standing on his own feet. That's a relief. Now I can focus on my sweet daughter, Denise, and my precious little Chi Chi! I know Kevin must be looking down from Heaven with his old friend Marshmallow and he's as pleased as a pumpkin." Jennifer recites this speech with dramatic enthusiasm, as if a Shakespeare soliloquy.

The short, red-haired man, someone who's been kind to the couple, can only nod at this barrage. The dog starts licking his face, and he finally makes excuses.

Jennifer heads straight to Finley and Andrea's pew. "I'm so excited for the wedding! I'm Finley's stepmother."

"Charmed, I'm sure. Thank you so much for taking care of the rehearsal dinner." Andrea smiles rather strained.

"I'm looking forward to it! I haven't been to Sizzler in ages." Chi Chi begins to wriggle out of Jennifer's arms, but she takes hold of her paw and bounces the Chihuahua up and down. "It's okay, little baby. *Shhhh...*"

Andrea hides her disdain of buffets and Chihuahuas. Finley knows she made it clear that Sizzler was positively out of the question. Yet Jennifer had blazed ahead and booked the buffet restaurant anyway.

"Sizzler? Now that's what I'm talking about," Joey says, walking up the aisle. "How about a hug for your favorite cousin? Wait 'til you see your mother. She looks fantastic. And here's Aunt Desiree."

Andrea hasn't seen Desiree in years and looks at the powdered face, hazel eyes peering through eyeglasses.

Finley can smell the Chanel No. 5 and notices she's wearing three cardigans with tiny pearls for buttons.

"So glad you're here!" Andrea gives her aunt a hug. "Where is Mother?"

Desiree nods at the church door. "She'll be in soon with your father. She's looking so much better every day!"

Robbie strides into the chapel, looking around as if he's found himself in a foreign country. He kisses Andrea's hand. "The lovely bride. And who is your beautiful friend?"

"I'm her Aunt Desiree."

Robbie turns to Andrea. "I've arranged for an entertainer to jazz up the dinner. Is it okay if she watches the rehearsal? She showed up early. She's all set up at Sizzler."

Andrea stares. "What kind of entertainer?"

"You're gonna love her act. If you do, she'll reprise her starring role at the reception. You've heard of Heidi Holt? She's performed on my show a couple times, and she's killing it."

"She always wears the silver-sequined top hat?" Andrea asks. "And she gets that Maltese to jump through a fiery hoop? Oh my God, that makes Sizzler more bearable. Thank you, Robbie!" Andrea gives Robbie an unexpected bear hug. She whispers in his ear, "See if you can make that dog over there, Chi Chi, part of the act."

"I'll see what I can do." Robbie sits as soon as he sees Finley and the officiant, a seasoned Elvis impersonator, approaching the front.

Andrea turns her eyes back to the door after she hears rustling sounds.

A middle-aged woman with an angled nose and brown hair struggles to bring an oversized cardboard box into the room. Her butter-colored blouse over a beige skirt and leather boots looks stylish, even as she fumbles.

Andrea recognizes her mother and rushes over to help.

Finley sees Scott turn pale in his pew, clutching Mr. Sparkle's hand.

"My beautiful Andrea!" Lorraine sets the box on the carpet and squeezes her daughter.

"So wonderful to see you! What could be in this box?" Andrea can't stop her natural curiosity.

"I made flower wreaths for your bridesmaids in out-patient therapy," Lorraine says in wispy singsong.

Andrea looks at the purple wreaths, pretty in a bohemian way. Purple is one of the wedding colors; her mother got that right. The wreaths are the most un-Versace accessory imaginable, and Andrea knows she cannot allow her chic bridesmaids to wear them, but her eyes fill with tears.   Her mother did something loving.

She can't stop crying, and the tear drops land on the cardboard box. She can't believe her emotion, and she steadies herself with a hand on the pew. She's about to make the biggest sartorial sacrifice of her life. "Mother... Mother, these are so perfect. I think the flower girls should wear them."

Finley notices his fiancée crying and rushes over. He pats her shoulders for a minute and holds her until the crying slows.

"It's okay. I'm just really happy and overwhelmed."

The group arrives in batches at Sizzler. Andrea and Finley get to the restaurant first and wait at an empty table. They love getting some time to themselves after a dramatic rehearsal. Finley feels a chill up his spine as he hears his stepmother and half-sister on speaker phone, getting louder.

Jennifer approaches the table. She sits without looking at Andrea or Finley. "Oh, honey! I'm so proud of you! You've got three jobs to choose from... Of course, you'll do fabulously at any one of them. You're the first electrical engineer in our family! The smartest one in the family. And you're also a beautiful dancer and artist. A Renaissance woman."

"Thanks, Mom!" Denise answers over the phone. "There are so many opportunities and only one me. Is Finley there? Can I talk to my big bro?"

"Oh yes, we're on speaker." Jennifer motions with her manicured hand to Finley.

"Hello. We're at Sizzler."

"Finley! It's Denise. You can call me Didi. How are you? I'm so happy for you! I wish I could be there, but you know how it is. May I speak to the lovely bride?"

"Hi, this is Andrea."

"You're so lucky to be at Sizzler. It's my favorite place. I don't eat meat, but the green beans really sizzle. And the foiled baked potatoes, my goodness. Have you met Chi Chi?"

"She's a Chihuahua all right," Andrea deadpans. Finley laughs.

"So, what are you and my brother up to? What do you do? What does Finley do? I know he's an actor..."

"I manage business for my father. He created the *Mr. Glitz* comic. Finley." Andrea pats her fiancé's back "Finley has made a movie splash in his first film, *Fidelity*, and we're both headed to Spain after the honeymoon for the next movie, *Assassination of a Bullfighter*."

"What was the *Mr. Glitz* comic? Was he that little bald guy? That was so whimsical."

"I think you're thinking of the Ziggy character. Mr. Glitz is a glamorous orangutan. The strip was mostly local, but there was a Saturday morning cartoon..."

"Wow. I love orangutans. They've got such furry arms," Denise says, but Andrea stares at the phone in awkward silence. "My brother has been busy. Well, congratulations, you two! Would you mind putting Mom back on the line?"

"No problem." Andrea turns to her menu and leans on an elbow.

"Denise, what's going on with Jake and your adorable baby?" Jennifer continues on speaker phone.

"Oh, Little Kevin took his first steps. His pediatrician says he seems very verbal for his age. We're over the moon."

"How wonderful. I should let you go now because this rehearsal dinner's starting. Tell Little Kevin that Grammie loves him. And I love you, too. You're my sunshine, my only sunshine! I'll be home very soon. Bye, sweetie. Love you."

"Bye, Mommy. Come home soon!"

Jennifer turns her phone off and faces Andrea with a stretched social smile.

Andrea and Finley fall silent, and Jennifer soon heads over to the buffet table.

Finley remembers the Chihuahua and breaks the silence. "Where is Chi Chi, by the way?"

"Oh, I hired a dogsitter I found through The Laga Brutto. She's pampering my little queen tonight. She even chauffeured little Chi Chi back to her room." Jennifer beams at the thought of Chi Chi lounging on her velvet cushion.

"Excuse me." Finley sees Provocateur and someone at the front of the restaurant, eying each other with unease. The relative holds an enormous gold present. "Is that one of your relative's standing with Provocateur?"

"It's Cousin Joey! One of my cousin Joeys, that is." Andrea smiles. "Let's go say hello. And rescue the restaurant before they start arguing with each other. God forbid they start talking about your Castro movie."

"What would Joey say about *Fidelity*?"

"He'd say it was un-American Commie bullshit," Andrea says without a trace of doubt.

"Thanks for letting me know." Finley motions for Provocateur to come sit at the table while Joey and Andrea catch up. "May I introduce the distinguished director of film, Provocateur?" Finley asks Jennifer.

"Hello." She eyes the man in a bandana and guyliner with wary eyes, but extends her hand.

"Charmed, madame." He kisses the hand instead of shaking it, and Finley sees a fleeting look of disgust cross his stepmother's face. He can't help but smile and forces himself not to laugh. "I am to be a groomsman at the wedding, but I could not be present at the rehearsal due to an intense meditative sequence in the desert."

"How interesting. I'm Finley's stepmother, Jennifer."

Andrea and Joey arrive at the table, and Finley can just make out the end of an argument about the Mets. Robbie enters the room, ushering Heidi Holt over to discuss her performance with Sizzler management.

She's outfitted in a sparkly, black bodysuit, heels, and tuxedo jacket. Her blonde hair is mostly hidden under her top hat in an upswept style. She approaches the table. She pulls a bouquet of roses out of her jacket and hands it to Andrea with a magician's flourish.

"Thank you." Andrea loves roses.

"Congratulations to the lovely couple! Do I have any volunteers I can saw in half? You could both participate as a couple, you know."

"I'm sure Finley wouldn't mind, but I'm wearing Versace, so...I'll have to take a raincheck." Andrea smooths the red satin fabric on her lap.

"Yes, ma'am. I'll take good care of the groom, don't worry. I have a surgeon's license in addition to my magic license. I have another special trick up my hat planned for him." Heidi winks at Finley. "And my assistant tonight is the lovely Robbie Roberts."

Jennifer returns to set her vegetable-laden plate on the table. "You must be Heidi. Lovely costume." She touches a flower on Heidi's lapel, and it squirts her. She blinks. "Oh!"

"Always be on the lookout for a magician's boutonniere, ma'am. But don't worry, I'm all out of whoopee cushions." Heidi looks at Jennifer's unsmiling face. "And I'm here until midnight."

Finley laughs out loud, and Andrea squeezes his hand. *Maybe the rehearsal dinner won't be a disaster after all.* He sees Robbie approaching with a bottle of champagne.

"For the lovely bride-to-be." Robbie smiles at Andrea and hands her the Veuve Clicquot with a leopard-print bow. "Excuse me, I'm going to help Heidi set up her stage. I am her assistant. It's a side gig. Come with me, lovely Heidi."

"Those rabbits aren't going to pull themselves out of my hat. I'll see you all soon, during my electrifying performance!" Heidi waves her wand and disappears in a puff of purple smoke.

Everyone applauds.

Desiree looks startled at the smoke as she leads her sister Lorraine towards the table. They both place beautiful floral-wrapped presents in front of Andrea. Desiree looks at Andrea with surprise. "You got a magician?"

"This is a Vegas rehearsal dinner, you know. Anything can happen. But never mind that. It's so great to see my aunt and my mother. I hope you're enjoying your room at The Laga Brutto."

"It's very luxurious, but the walls are too thin. I think I could hear the couple next to us all night—"

"Maybe I can talk to the manager and get you moved to another room," Andrea interrupts before her mother can share the gory details.

"I may have seen them checking out. They were a lovely couple, but he had so many tattoos, and her heels were so high. Kind of trashy. They kept screaming at each other all the way down the hall," Desiree chimes in.

Andrea laughs. "There's always something going on, isn't there?"

"It's just hard... It's hard to go to sleep with thin walls. It reminds me of rehab. Did you know I was in rehab? There were so many people doing the hanky-panky and sneaking into rooms... I can't go back there." Lorraine doesn't notice Jennifer paling or Provocateur's raised eyebrow.

"I'll see what I can do. Don't worry, Mother, you're not going back to rehab. You've got this." Andrea squeezes her mother's hand.

An awkward silence descends on the group. Then, Andrea looks over to the enormous glass doors and smiles. Her maid of honor has arrived with voluminous gift bags.

Finley knows her only as Tanya Rose and never sees her much; he only knows that Andrea will disappear with her for hours on end for shopping or lunch or a spa day. He notices a man walking through the door. He realizes it's Jeremy Berry. He knows Jeremy is trying to make it as a country singer, but he didn't expect the cowboy hat and guitar were going to become permanent accessories. Finley still can't believe how much tanner and more muscular Jeremy looks since high school. His dark, dramatic eyebrows and deep-set brown eyes always made him a hit with the girls, and Finley can imagine Jeremy playing up that charm in Nashville. "Jeremy, great to see you again! You made it." Finley shakes his hand then gives him a hug.

"I'd never miss your wedding, man. I still can't understand why I'm not the best man." Jeremy crosses his arms in mock anger.

"Robbie was local, you know. That's all it was. I couldn't ask you to plan everything from Nashville. You have to admit, Robbie put on one hell of a bachelor party."

Jeremy strums his guitar. "It's great to be here in Las Vegas. I scored a few gigs while I'm here, but I want to make time for my best friend. I missed out on a lot since you left Nashville, but I'm going to make it up to you. Right here, right now. I'm here to serenade you and your lovely bride-to-be." He starts tuning his guitar at the table.

"Now is a great time. I mean, before the magic show starts.... I'll bring Andrea back." Finley walks to the glass doors and enormous cactus by the window. "Sorry to interrupt. My best friend from high school wants to serenade us."

"This, I've got to hear." Andrea grins, and Tanya lifts her plucked eyebrows to such a degree that one of her false eyelashes wiggle.

Everyone sits at a table that is becoming increasingly full. Tanya places a vase of lavender roses and lilies as a centerpiece.

Jeremy strums his guitar once more. "You know, my dream is to become a country music legend. And as I'm building up a following in my hometown of Nashville, I'll always stay close to my roots and to those special friends like Finley who believed in me, who supported me. He always saw the raw talent inside me. I'm mighty honored to be here to celebrate this very special romantic occasion, so I sat down, and I wrote a song. This is an original composition, and I call it, 'On a Chestnut Day.' The thing about it is, the chestnut tree in the field at our school was where me and Finley would practice our harmonies after lunch. Other guys were cutting up, but we were making music with our other friend who couldn't be here today, Jessie. Jessie had an accident last Tuesday, riding his ATV with his son Andy, but he's healing and getting better every day. I'm sure they'll even take his stitches out this week. I want to dedicate this song to Finley and Andrea." He plays an introduction, and Jeremy sings in a twangy sort of baritone:

"When we say them vows,
On a wedding day,
The perfect breeze
And the bales of hay.
We'll ride away
On a chestnut day

To a country field
And we'll make it real,
We'll seal the deal,
When a man in cowboy hat
Loves a lady love
To his dying day,
And they run away
To spread their love
On a chestnut day
On a chestnut day."

He finishes the song with a flourish on guitar.

Lorraine's clouded hazel eyes fill with tears while Tanya looks unimpressed, and Provocateur looks at Jeremy quizzically.

Finley claps for his friend, and the rest of the party joins him.

"Very nice." Andrea nods and smiles, but Finley can't be sure if she enjoyed the song, or if she's only being polite.

"That was beautiful. You've really got a voice, and you're a handsome cowboy." Lorraine pats Jeremy's hand for a while.

Provocateur clears his throat. "Finley, I didn't know you were from Nashville. I didn't get a chance to talk to Jeremy much at the bachelor party."

"Born and raised. But I moved to Downey, California, after high school...and then Vegas. You know the rest of the story. Now, it's back to L.A. again."

Provocateur grasps his water glass, lost in thought. "I've always had a fascination with Nashville. The dichotomies abound. Ragged Americana mingles with the decay of the bourgeois in all its poverties of minutia... Maybe we should work on a country music film in the future. You know, country is the most popular radio format in the United States. I've got a script about doomed lovers set in the opera world of the 16th century, but we could change the setting to modern-day Nashville."

"I'm not sure what you mean about Nashville, but it's a great place to make a movie. You could film it at the Grand Ole Opry!" Jeremy considers the idea with enthusiasm. "But maybe the lovers should have a happy ending."

"Let's just focus on the wedding and not the next movie right now. We haven't even started production on *The Assassination of a Bullfighter*." Finley laughs, but he knows Provocateur never forgets an idea.

"Bullfighter? Hell, I always thought you'd join the rodeo someday, Finley."

"I've never seen a rodeo. I've never even been to Nashville," Lorraine whimpers.

"Well, maybe Finley should visit sometime, and he can bring the whole family with him. There's nothing like a Nashville Christmas. Did you know The Opryland Resort has thousands of poinsettias every year? And it's free admission for anyone. And Finley always loved that Festival of Christmas Trees at Cheekwood Estate. Our high school even decorated a tree one year. But Finley almost fell off the ladder trying to put the angel on top."

"You can stop now, Jeremy." Finley glares.

"I think your new family needs to know the whole story. They need to know what they're really getting into here. I brought lots of old high school photos. Remember Coach Harris and that game we lost? I've got all the evidence with me. And I hope Andrea isn't the jealous type because I've got the prom photos of me and Laurie and you and Carla, too. And your first old Mustang. And that time you shaved your head. When it grew back, everybody in the hallway kept trying to touch the peach fuzz on your head." Jeremy displays the photo of a bald teenage Finley with a group of teenagers in a Taco Bell parking lot.

"Jesus Christ! That's amazing." Andrea laughs. "Please don't shave your head again." She takes on a more serious look. "Does balding run in your family?"

Jennifer leans forward. "I hate to spill my husband's secrets, but Kevin wore a small toupee when he got older."

"Oh no." Finley looks horrified at the thought of a receding hairline.

"Well, your grandfather and that cousin that took us fishing had a full head of hair," Jeremy tries to make his friend feel better. "And you could always get a cowboy hat, like me, if you did go bald."

"Maybe he could wear a beret instead. Or a bandana," Provocateur suggests.

"I'm not bald yet, okay? And let's get back on track. I think the magic show is starting. Heidi Holt looks like she's ready." Finley looks towards the front of the restaurant, where Heidi has set up a stage for her performance.

"Ladies and Gentlemen! Behold, the unprecedented, the unimaginable Heidi Holt! She will astound you with magic," Robbie announces.

"For my first trick, I'll take a rabbit out of a hat." Heidi waves her wand over a top hat she's just removed from her head. "Oh no, something went wrong." She pulls out a plush version of Marshmallow. "Here, I think this rabbit belongs to you." She hands the rabbit to Finley. "Let's try one more time." She waves the wand a few more times over the upside-down hat. "That's some bunny!" She takes out a huge, live, lop-eared bunny. "I'll let my assistant handle this."

Robbie hands the rabbit to a bearded man who walks out the door.

Heidi turns her attention to a deck of cards. "Pick a card, any card."

Andrea picks.

"Remember your card. But don't tell me what it is. Reshuffle the deck, please." Heidi takes the deck back and pulls out a card. "Was this your card...The Queen of Hearts?"

Andrea laughs, "You got me. It was the Queen of Hearts."

"This is a sign of love and happiness for years to come. Please, everyone, applaud this couple! For my big finale, Heidi Holt will disappear in a puff of smoke!"

No sooner does she finish speaking then she disappears, leaving behind purple smoke.

Robbie walks forward to the edge of the stage. "Let's hear it for Heidi Holt! Tickets are now available for Heidi's Evening of Magic at The Realm of Venus every Saturday night, now through February!"

FINLEY MAKES AN ENTRANCE

Andrea looks around Elvis Chapel, wondering where the groom is. She eyes someone in a Mr. Glitz suit rearranging HER flowers. He's even stumbling a bit, drunk before happy hour starts. Goddamn it, had that dancer crashed the wedding? She hands Tonya Rose her bouquet and stomps in her Versace heels straight towards the metaphorical fly in her calla lilies. "Are you that addict I fired? You're not getting a paycheck if that's why you're here! That was a year ago. You really are insane. Get some help."

"Actually, I think I'm right on time." Finley takes off the orangutan head. "Are you really set on marrying a monkey like me?"

"There'd better be a Dolce & Gabbana tux under there, Finley!"

Indeed, there is a tuxedo. Finley cleans up nicely. "I'd better go wait for my bride to walk down the aisle."

"Ummm...what's going on ? Isn't it bad luck to see the bride before the wedding?" Scott interrupts. He looks at the orangutan suit with a puzzled stare. "If I'm interrupting a...personal moment, forgive me, but we did plan a wedding today." Scott adjusts his bowtie and sweeps invisible lint off the cuffs of his ruffled yet understated tuxedo shirt.

Finley takes Andrea's hand in his. "I wanted to remind you of the Christmas show. That I'll always be your hero."

Scott sighs, and interrupts again. "That's sweet in a strange way, but I'm not sure who's saving who in your relationship."

"Dad. Stop. Give us a moment. And straighten your calla lily." She adjusts the large boutonnière on his aubergine jacket. "And check if the candles are lit."

Scott stops her hand and kisses her forehead. "Try to relax. You'll be married soon." He walks over to the chapel's Elvis impersonator, leaving Andrea to deal with Finley.

Andrea glares at her husband-to-be with a potent mix of emotions and balls her fists at her sides, but she can't help smiling. Finley tried to pull off a romantic gesture. She blows him a kiss. "Baby, if I wanted a hero, I could marry a firefighter or something."

Finley opens his mouth to defend himself, but then closes it. He winks instead. "Hurry up. Let's get married."

Andrea disappears into the chapel's larger room. Finley waits a moment then follows her.

The party waits for their officiant, and The King doesn't disappoint. He begins the ceremony by singing "Love Me Tender."

Finley watches as Provocateur walks the first bridesmaid down the aisle: Andrea's friend from high school, Tiffany. Next comes Jeremy Berry, wearing his ever-present cowboy hat with the white tuxedo Andrea chose for the occasion. Jeremy exchanges glances with the bridesmaid on his arm, a red-haired woman who Andrea often shops with around Vegas, Heather. Last of all, Robbie Roberts walks the maid of honor, Tonya Rose, down the aisle.

All eyes turn towards the front of the chapel. Mr. Sparkle and Scott walk Andrea down the aisle. Andrea stops in front of Lorraine. Andrea pulls out a white rose from the stunning, ball-shaped bouquet and gives it to her mother.

Finley knows he has a stunning bride, but Andrea looks like a fairytale vision in a sparkling, hand-beaded mermaid dress. The strapless dress shows off her beautiful tan and her shoulders. He hair flows downward with the veil and her makeup is somehow glamorous and natural.

At the end of the aisle, Chas lifts the veil, and Andrea stands before Finley. They join hands and repeat the vows as

Elvis instructs, but Finley can't remember the words coming out of his own mouth and feels as if he is in a waking dream.

The Elvis impersonator smiles. "I now pronounce you man and wife. You may kiss your bride!"

Finley forgets the people around them, forgets Elvis's strong cologne, and forgets everything except Andrea's lips. He doesn't want to stop kissing her and feels Andrea's hand drifting near his thigh. He presses the kiss a bit harder, but then regains composure. He pulls back a bit.

Andrea looks at him. She whispers, "Is my lipstick smeared?"

"You look perfect."

"I'll have to touch up for photos."

Elvis sings "Viva Las Vegas" to finish out the ceremony.

As they ride in the limousine, Finley kisses his bride over and over again. "We're really married. And we're moving to a little bungalow. And I'm a movie star with a beautiful wife. And we're going to Spain. I didn't think any of this would happen when I met you. I wasted so much of my life feeling bitter about the past. I didn't get enough of my Dad's attention. Life wasn't fair... But, *The Marshmallow Show* being canceled was the best thing that's ever happened to me. Because now, we're married and moving forward. It may sound corny, but we've only just begun."

"You were always a diamond in the rough. You just needed time to see it. And a woman to show you. And let's dial back the movie star stuff. You're a working actor." She winks at her new husband. "Wait until you see what the wedding planner created for us at The Laga Brutto. It's a *Swan Lake* theme! The groom's cake is in your favorite flavor, caramel, but it's shaped like a swan. There're white-feathered floral arrangements on each table. And I'm sure our cake is one of the largest wedding cakes in Vegas history. It's almost as tall as Elvis and Priscilla's cake!"

"I hope I actually get a chance to eat a lot of cake. I know the reception can get busy."

Never has there been quite the couple as Finley and Andrea walking into the party at Laga Brutto, or a cake quite so massive. They sit for a while at their couple's table but soon find themselves making the rounds to talk to everyone.

The multi-course Italian menu begins with a chilled salad and antipasto. Even his fork feels frigid to the touch, marvels Finley. Meanwhile, Andrea focuses on the golden swans made of flowers.

Finley feels restless. The wedding party plans to participate in a toast to the happy couple, but Jeremy Berry and Heather have disappeared.

Robbie walks over to Finley. "Do you know where Jeremy is? It's almost time for the toast." Robbie clears his throat and leans forward, conspiratorial. "He might be a few...minutes. I saw Jeremy and that bridesmaid going into a bathroom together. They were kissing."

Finley's jaw drops. He knows his best friend is a ladies' man, but he hadn't expected this course of events. "No problem. We'll just delay things a bit. Maybe you can get your speech going early and just keep talking until we see them walk into the ballroom."

"I am a talk show host. I can make a speech anywhere. Alright, you got it." Robbie clinks a fork on his champagne glass. He waits a minute for the chatter to die down. "It's the moment you've all been waiting for: my speech. But, I know tonight isn't about the celebrity Robbie Roberts or my legendary talk show, *Robbie Roberts Tonight!* It's about a very special couple, Andrea and Finley. When I first met Finley, he was a mess. He barged his way into the green room, and he wouldn't leave. But then, the cameras started to roll, and some magic happened that day. He didn't create Marshmallow, but he took her in a new, more mature direction. She's like if Joan Rivers merged with Miss Piggy and became a rabbit. I hired Finley out of pity—and also because he had some talent. But then, something happened. He fell in love."

Robbie pauses as he notices an older man with a beard approaching the table, looking straight at him.

"May I help you, sir? I don't know if you've noticed, but we're having a wedding reception here. If you want an autograph, I'd be happy to arrange that at a later date."

"You can help me, yes. I'm a relative of Finley's and we've met before. I tried to stay quiet, but then you got up here and opened your damn mouth. And I can't stand it. I can't stand it another minute." The man balls his hands into fists.

Finley's mouth drops, and he responds, "Dad? You're dead, I mean... Oh my God."

"I am very much alive," Kevin Luker says. "I had to fake my death, or that bitch Jennifer over there would have spent all my money, and California law would have let her. And a divorce would have been even more expensive. Old Jeff Savoie was kind enough to let me stay on his private island." Kevin pauses, as if trying to find words.

The room has become silent.

Mr. Sparkle sits at the end of the main table, mopping his forehead with a monogrammed handkerchief. An older woman in a dark purple gown drops a dinner fork and an enormous salad falls with it. A harried server rushes over to clean up the mess. The clatter seems unbearable, but then silence resumes.

Kevin stares down the hostile crowd and resumes his tirade. "I turn on my television—Did you know that television is a simple joy of life? And I see my Marshmallow on that drug addict's TV show. How could you do that to me?" Kevin looks at his son, who remains silent. "And he's your best man? And you're making movies with a Communist?" Kevin emphasizes each syllable of Communist while angrily pointing at Provocateur. "I sent Savoie over to your pathetic film headquarters, and he could not believe his eyes. I tried to get you a real movie, Finley. Savoie was going to offer you a role, so you'd have a real career. But you turned him down for this...this Provocateur person over here. He doesn't even have a real name." Kevin stares at Provocateur with boiling rage.

The director says nothing and smiles back in an amused way, further enraging Finley's father.

Kevin continues his ranting, looking back at his son, "I can't stop you from throwing your life away. But I came back, even though it could cost me millions, to get Marshmallow off

Robbie Robert's disgusting show. I never would have agreed for my Marshmallow to ever appear on that show again. And it's going to stop. It's going to stop right now. You will never be Marshmallow again if I have anything to do with it." Kevin pauses to take a breath.

Andrea stands, white with rage. "Are you finished? Are you done? I'd say so. Finley told me his dad wasn't the best father, but you have exceeded my expectations. And as far as Marshmallow is concerned, you signed her over to my father's company before your not-so-real death. I own that goddamn bunny, and there's nothing you can do about it. You would risk jail just to ruin your son's wedding? You are sick. Sick, in my opinion. I've gotten to know your son and Robbie Roberts—the only problem here is you." She stares at her father-in-law, but he remains silent.

Finley stands up straight, a sad expression on his face. He puts his arm around Andrea.

She nods towards him as if to encourage him.

It's his turn to speak.

"You know what, Dad? I've got characters of my own. Robbie even likes a few of them. Maybe I will never be Marshmallow again. That's fine with me. Wasn't she really just a mouthpiece for all your bullshit? And let's face it, she was your favorite child. But she's not real. People are more important than imaginary characters. That's what I've learned these last two years. And don't you ever say another word about my friends again. We'd all appreciate if you would just leave. If everything you say is true, then you're guilty of numerous crimes, including trespassing an event."

"You'll be hearing from my lawyers. Many of you will be hearing from my lawyers. And that goes for you... Jennifer." Kevin turns on his heel and stalks out of the ballroom, grabbing a gift bag on his way out.

"You son of a bitch!" Jennifer screams from her seat at her departing husband. She rushes after him, and they both disappear from the ballroom.

Joey rushes after Kevin to share his sentiments. "You're lucky this is a classy wedding, pal. I'd like to give you a fat lip. Next time, stay dead! We like you better that way!"

Joey turns to Andrea. "Are you okay? Don't worry about that guy. He's a piece of work."

Andrea nods and looks at Finley. He gives her a kiss. Joey comes in for a hug along with Chas, Scott, Desiree, Lorraine, and Tonya Rose. "We love you. Your reception is amazing. You're an angel," Scott reassures her, then looks at Finley. "Maybe I was wrong earlier. Maybe you are a hero."

Finley can't find words. He gives Scott a sudden hug. He may have lost his own father, but his new father-in-laws are definitely a consolation. Chas looks at them, puzzled, still grasping his handkerchief.

Jeremy and Heather walk into the ballroom a few minutes later, their clothes rumpled. Heather's hair has started to come undone. Jeremy looks wide-eyed at the departing figure of Kevin Luker and the silent crowd sitting at their tables. "Did I miss something?"

Finley just shakes his head and sits down.

Robbie grabs the microphone and resumes his speech. "After hearing that, my respect for Finley and how hard he's worked to become the man he is today has only grown stronger. I am more than proud to be his best man."

The crowd starts to applaud and then they give Robbie a standing ovation.

"I'd also like to respond to the accusations that Kevin Luker hurled at me. I did interview the man years ago, and I was an asshole. I felt so guilty about it that I even brought it up at a group therapy meeting. But now I don't feel guilty anymore. He didn't really die, so that means I'm off the hook. I can't speak to his statement that I am disgusting; that's an opinion, but I consider myself a recovering drug addict. I'm giving group therapy a try. And maybe I'll even seek other treatment. Stay tuned. And speaking of staying tuned, tune into *Robbie Roberts Tonight!* Maybe I'll score the first interview with Finley about having a zombie for a father."

Robbie waits for his joke to land.

Some of the tension eases out the room.

He takes a swig of champagne. "I'd like to officially announce that Finley Luker is no longer recurring on *Robbie Roberts Tonight!* I'm promoting him to featured performer.

That means a dressing room and a parking space in Hollywood."

The announcement gets polite applause.

"Okay, he can be a sidekick. Sometimes. But enough about me, ladies and gentlemen. I think it's time we heard from the other groomsmen." Robbie hands Jeremy the microphone.

Jeremy takes off his cowboy hat. "I don't know what I walked in on, and I'm not sure I want to know. And I'd like to add that, in all the time I've spent with Robbie Roberts over there, not once did I see him use an illegal substance. We've all got a cross to bear. For some of us, it's addiction, but today is a celebration of love. Finley and Andrea have graciously shared their special day with us, and I am mighty proud to be part of it. I've written a song, and, with your permission, I'd like to sing it. I want to thank Finley for his support and the support of the Las Vegas community." Jeremy sets the microphone on its stand and puts the cowboy hat back onto his head.

Finley wonders if Jeremy is going to sing acapella, but a guitar seems to appear from under the table.

Jeremy strums a few bars and begins to sing:
"For we know, every man's a cowboy
When it comes to a woman's love.
And they'll build a home together,
And fill the world with a cowboy's love.
Take my hand, we'll ride away now
On a white horse riding to the sea.
There'll be no more prairie between us
In this land for you and me."

Jeremy plays the ending notes on guitar. "Thank you, you've been a great audience. I'll be performing at The Silver Rush on Fremont Street tomorrow at 9PM. I'd love to see you there."

Provocateur heads over to the microphone. He stands with perfect posture and looks around the room. "I'd also like to address statements made by the uninvited guest. I do not consider myself a Communist in the Marxist sense, but I understand why many intelligent people abhor Capitalism. The harsh inequalities of our society leave many persons without food or housing. The film that I created as an auteur director with Finley explores the character of the Communist leader of Cuba, Fidel Castro. I leave it to the viewer to decide what to make of it, but the film is art. It is not a political statement." Provocateur turns towards the groom. "As for this man, he will begin work on my new film, *The Assassination of a Bullfighter*. Noone but Finley can portray my tapestry of vision. I am honored to know him. Remember, though he has suffered tonight, his journey is only beginning. Thank you." Provocateur puts the mic back in its stand.

Bringing the unconventional wedding back to order, DJ Gouda announces, "Time for the father-daughter dance."

Chas and Andrea rehearsed for weeks, but now Chas seems bolted to his seat. He shakes his head. Chas gestures to his husband and Andrea, who's still clutching his handkerchief.

Scott straightens his bowtie and holds out a hand to Andrea. They stand on the dance floor, overshadowed by the enormous floral swan arrangement on the stage. Gouda hits a button on the soundboard. The opening notes of "What a Wonderful World" begin, and the two dance with undeniable rhythm. Scott leads the dance in an intuitive way, predicting choreography and adding his own twist. As the song ends, Scott dips Andrea for a strong finish. She seems surprised, but the two execute the maneuver in style.

Although not all the guests stick around after the wedding exploded, strong applause rings out.

Andrea and Scott take a bow.

Gouda returns to the mic. "It is a wonderful world, ladies and gentlemen. And now, time for the mother-son dance!"

Finley walks up to the stage, unsure. He hasn't seen his stepmother, Jennifer, since she ran after his father. He steps towards the DJ to tell him that he doesn't have a partner but stops when he sees his father-in-law moving onto the dance floor.

Chas guides Lorraine in front of his new son-in-law.

Finley steps into position as Jennifer's chosen song plays. Lorraine looks confused as she hears the Macarena, but does her best to remember the dance. Finley soon tires of the repetitive silliness, but he notices Lorraine's happy smile.

The audience laughs and applauds as the song finishes.

Andrea rushes over to her mother. "Thank you, Mommy."

Lorraine's eyes mist with tears and she grips Andrea's hand for a moment before returning to her table.

"Well, ladies and gentlemen, we're just getting the party started. Please put on your boogie shoes and dance the Electric Slide! The dance floor is open!"

Andrea walks over and whispers in Gouda's ear. Gouda clears his throat to announce, "Correction. I've had a song request from the bride. Take that special someone to the floor because we have a slow one for you folks."

Andrea grabs Finley and leads him out to the floor. It's a very slow song, a Robert Goulet standard that Scott loves, "If Ever I Would Leave You." They have no difficulty conversing as they dance to the beat and hold each other close. "I'm so sorry about what your father just did to you." Andrea has a tear in her eye. "It was so cruel."

"It's okay. I'm at peace with it. He made me realize that I was wasting my time all these years trying to earn his approval. I was never going to get it. Besides, I have a new family now. And I love you."

"I love you, Finley Luker."

Thanks for reading! Find more transgressive fiction (poems, novels, anthologies) at: Outcast-Press.com

Twitter & Instagram: @OutcastPress, @OutcastPress1

Facebook.com/OutcastPress1

Email proof of your Amazon/GoodReads review to OutcastPressSubmissions@gmail.com & we'll mail you a free bookmark & stickers!

Teenage dreams, rebellion & coming-of-age irony. *Modernist Dreams Brutalist Nightmares* is a searingly honest & brutally funny account of LG Thomson's experience as part of the first generation to grow up in Scotland's most ambitious New Town. From Glasgow to a council house in Cumbernauld, she grows up in a post-WWII social experiment billed as The Town for Tomorrow.

More From Outcast Press

Cracker, the explosive sequel to *Poser,* is here to answer what *Desperate Housewives* would be like written by Quinten Tarantino. In this noir romance sprinkled with ecstasy pills, pearl-handled guns, and secret alliance, Ambrose fights through jealousy, grief, and a trip to Texas to reconnect with his imprisoned little bro, Butch. When Ambrose returns to the Bay Area, he faces a showdown with the men who've been antagonizing his caring dominatrix boss and her dungeon, Dover, Inc..

Acknowledgments

Writing my first novel was wonderful, but I didn' t get there alone. Early influences include Mrs. Todd, who introduced *Charlotte' s Web* to me, Mrs. Wall who was the first teacher to notice me in a positive way, and my high school English teacher, Mr. Qualls, who taught me to diagram sentences.

I want to thank the ladies of the Huffman Book Rack, the used bookstore on the long walk home from school. I didn' t always buy a book, but the ladies always welcomed me.

My brother, Daniel, will always be the first person who discusses books with me.

I' d like to thank my husband, Jim, for buying me a MacBook Air for Christmas and a million things I can' t verbalize here.

I' d like to thank the attendees of Huntsville Pub Crawls, who listen to my monologues about literature without complaint. I want to thank Dr. Pukis for prescribing Wellbutrin to help me with depression after my mother' s death. I' d never been able to sustain a long narrative before this. He knew I' d had bad experiences with psychiatric drugs in the past, but assured me, "This is a different class of drug." He was right and thank God.

Then there' s Grant Ginder. I hadn' t liked any new novels in a very long time until *The People We Hate at the Wedding*. He responded to my post about the book on Instagram and tweeted about a Catapult class on character development he was teaching during COVID-19. I thought, why not? Although Zooming with a handsome, accomplished, "very gay" author was terrifying, I learned from it.

I'd like to thank my friends Daniel and Amber for being wonderful and encouraging my writing.

I queried several publishers, then literary agents. I got one fairly positive rejection that contained the phrase "we aren't interested in publishing that kind of novel." I'd almost given until I saw Outcast Press on IG. A startling image of a beautiful woman hanging from a noose attached to floating balloons captivated me. I decided to query one more time. Did I expect a "yes"?

No.

After drinking a bit too much wine, I checked my email, and it wasn't a rejection! I couldn't believe it.

Special thanks go to Paige Johnson of Outcast Press. She's worked her magic on lots of more accomplished authors and it's amazing she was the final editor on my novel. Other luminaries of Outcast Press include Remo McCartney, who also edited *Marshmallow*. Although it is humbling that Remo has a better grasp of grammar, he imbued my work with coherence and made fabulous suggestions to complete ambiguous scenes.

Then there's Cody Sexton. He created a wonderful cover for *Marshmallow*. a twisted version of the cover of *Watership Down*.

And, finally, thanks to Sebastian Vice—firstly, for being named Sebastian Vice. He may be a living embodiment of my character, Provocateur, except Sebastian is a talented writer and not insane.

Thank you, thank you, Outcast Press!

About the Author

@DebBunny21

Debby Regan is a poet, mother, three-wheel bicycle enthusiast, and emotional support human to standard poodles. Although the Alabama-born writer has not yet fulfilled her dream of moving to New York City, she did marry a man from Queens who claims to be a rocket scientist. Her most recent published poem appears in the first edition of *Duck Duck Mongoose,* and she has a BA in English from The University of Alabama at Huntsville (UAH).